The Adventures of Sam Spade and Other Stories

MW00641336

Dashiell Hammett

Must Have Books
503 Deerfield Place
Victoria, BC
V9B 6G5
Canada

ISBN: 9781773237770

Copyright 2021 – Must Have Books

All rights reserved in accordance with international law. No part of this
book may be reproduced or transmitted in any form or by any means,
electronic or mechanical, including photocopying, recording, or by any
information storage or retrieval system, except in the case of excerpts by a
reviewer who may quote brief passages in an article or review, without written
permission from the publisher.

CONTENTS

Acknowledgment is gratefully made to the following magazines in which these stories originally appeared: BLACK MASK; COLLIER'S; THE AMERICAN MAGAZINE; MYSTERY LEAGUE. *The stories appear in their original form and have not been cut.*

TOO MANY HAVE LIVED

The man's tie was as orange as a sunset. He was a large man, tall and meaty, without softness. The dark hair parted in the middle, flattened to his scalp, his firm, full cheeks, the clothes that fit him with noticeable snugness, even the small, pink ears flat against the sides of his head—each of these seemed but a differently colored part of one same, smooth surface. His age could have been thirty-five or forty-five.

He sat beside Samuel Spade's desk, leaning forward a little over his Malacca stick, and said, "No. I want you to find out what happened to him. I hope you never find him." His protuberant green eyes stared solemnly at Spade.

Spade rocked back in his chair. His face—given a not unpleasantly satanic cast by the v's of his bony chin, mouth, nostrils, and thickish brows—was as politely interested as his voice. "Why?"

The green-eyed man spoke quietly, with assurance: "I can talk to you, Spade. You've the sort of reputation I want in a private detective. That's why I'm here."

Spade's nod committed him to nothing.

The green-eyed man said, "And any fair price is all right with me."

Spade nodded as before. "And with me," he said, "but I've got to know what you want to buy. You want to find out what's happened to this—uh—Eli Haven, but you don't care what it is?"

The green-eyed man lowered his voice, but there was no other change in his mien: "In a way I do. For instance, if you found him and fixed it so he stayed away for good, it might be worth more money to me."

"You mean even if he didn't want to stay away?"

The green-eyed man said, "Especially."

Spade smiled and shook his head. "Probably not enough more money—the way you mean it." He took his long, thick-fingered hands from the arms of his chair and turned their palms up. "Well, what's it all about, Colyer?"

Colyer's face reddened a little, but his eyes maintained their unblinking cold stare. "This man's got a wife. I like her. They had a row last week and he blew. If I can convince her he's gone for good, there's a chance she'll divorce him."

"I'd want to talk to her," Spade said. "Who is this Eli Haven? What does he do?"

"He's a bad egg. He doesn't do anything. Writes poetry or something."

"What can you tell me about him that'll help?"

"Nothing Julia, his wife, can't tell you. You're going to talk to her." Colyer stood up. "I've got connections. Maybe I can get something for you through them later." ...

4

A small-boned woman of twenty-five or -six opened the apartment door. Her powder-blue dress was trimmed with silver buttons. She was full-bosomed but slim, with straight shoulders and narrow hips, and she carried herself with a pride that would have been cockiness in one less graceful.

Spade said, "Mrs. Haven?"

She hesitated before saying "Yes."

"Gene Colyer sent me to see you. My name's Spade. I'm a private detective. He wants me to find your husband."

"And have you found him?"

"I told him I'd have to talk to you first."

Her smile went away. She studied his face gravely, feature by feature, then she said, "Certainly," and stepped back, drawing the door back with her.

When they were seated in facing chairs in a cheaply furnished room overlooking a playground where children were noisy, she asked, "Did Gene tell you why he wanted Eli found?"

"He said if you knew he was gone for good maybe you'd listen to reason."

She said nothing.

"Has he ever gone off like this before?"

"Often."

"What's he like?"

"He's a swell man," she said dispassionately, "when he's sober; and when he's drinking he's all right except with women and money."

"That leaves him a lot of room to be all right in. What does he do for a living?"

"He's a poet," she replied, "but nobody makes a living at that."

"Well?"

"Oh, he pops in with a little money now and then. Poker, races, he says. I don't know."

"How long've you been married?"

"Four years, almost"—he smiled mockingly.

"San Francisco all the time?"

"No, we lived in Seattle the first year and then came here."

"He from Seattle?"

She shook her head. "Some place in Delaware."

5

"What place?"

"I don't know."

Spade drew his thickish brows together a little. "Where are you from?"

She said sweetly, "You're not hunting for me."

"You act like it," he grumbled. "Well, who are his friends?"

"Don't ask me!"

He made an impatient grimace. "You know some of them," he insisted.

"Sure. There's a fellow named Minera and a Louis James and somebody he calls Conny."

"Who are they?"

"Men," she replied blandly. "I don't know anything about them. They phone or drop by to pick him up, or I see him around town with them. That's all I know."

"What do they do for a living? They can't all write poetry."

She laughed. "They could try. One of them, Louis James, is a—member of Gene's staff, I think. I honestly don't know any more about them than I've told you."

"Think they'd know where your husband is?"

She shrugged. "They're kidding me if they do. They still call up once in a while to see if he's turned up."

"And these women you mentioned?"

"They're not people I know."

Spade scowled thoughtfully at the floor, asked, "What'd he do before he started not making a living writing poetry?"

"Anything—sold vacuum cleaners, hoboed, went to sea, dealt blackjack, railroaded, canning houses, lumber camps, carnivals, worked on a newspaper—anything."

"Have any money when he left?"

"Three dollars he borrowed from me."

"What'd he say?"

She laughed. "Said if I used whatever influence I had with God while he was gone he'd be back at dinnertime with a surprise for me."

Spade raised his eyebrows. "You were on good terms?"

"Oh, yes. Our last fight had been patched up a couple of days before."

"When did he leave?"

6

"Thursday afternoon; three o'clock, I guess."

"Got any photographs of him?"

"Yes." She went to a table by one of the windows, pulled a drawer out, and turned towards Spade again with a photograph in her hand.

Spade looked at the picture of a thin face with deep-set eyes, a sensual mouth, and a heavily lined forehead topped by a disorderly mop of coarse blond hair.

He put Haven's photograph in his pocket and picked up his hat. He turned towards the door, halted. "What kind of poet is he? Pretty good?"

She shrugged. "That depends on who you ask."

"Any of it around here?"

"No." She smiled. "Think he's hiding between pages?"

"You never can tell what'll lead to what. I'll be back some time. Think things over and see if you can't find some way of loosening up a little more. 'By."

He walked down Post Street to Mulford's book store and asked for a volume of Haven's poetry.

"I'm sorry," the girl said. "I sold my last copy last week"—she smiled—"to Mr. Haven himself. I can order it for you."

"You know him?"

"Only through selling him books."

Spade pursed his lips, asked, "What day was it?" He gave her one of his business cards. "Please. It's important."

She went to a desk, turned the pages of a red-bound sales-book, and came back to him with the book open in her hand. "It was last Wednesday," she said, "and we delivered it to a Mr. Roger Ferris, 1981 Pacific Avenue."

"Thanks a lot," he said.

Outside, he hailed a taxicab and gave the driver Mr. Roger Ferris's address....

The Pacific Avenue house was a four-story, graystone one set behind a narrow strip of lawn. The room into which a plump-faced maid ushered Spade was large and high-ceiled.

Spade sat down, but when the maid had gone away he rose and began to walk around the room. He halted at a table where there were three books. One of them had a salmon-colored jacket on which was printed in red an outline drawing of a bolt of lightning striking the ground between a man and a woman, and in black the words *Colored Light, by Eli Haven.*

Spade picked up the book and went back to his chair.

7

There was an inscription on the flyleaf—heavy, irregular characters written with blue ink:

To good old Buck, who knew his colored lights, in memory of them there days. Eli

Spade turned pages at random and idly read a verse:

STATEMENT
Too many have livedAs we liveFor our lives to beProof of our living.
Too many have diedAs we dieFor their deaths to beProof of our dying.

He looked up from the book as a man in dinner clothes came into the room. He was not a tall man, but his erectness made him seem tall even when Spade's six feet and a fraction of an inch were standing before him. He had bright blue eyes undimmed by his fifty-some years, a sunburned face in which no muscle sagged, a smooth, broad forehead, and thick, short, nearly white hair. There was dignity in his countenance, and amiability.

He nodded at the book Spade still held. "How do you like it?"

Spade grinned, said, "I guess I'm just a mug," and put the book down. "That's what I came to see you about, though, Mr. Ferris. You know Haven?"

"Yes, certainly. Sit down, Mr. Spade." He sat in a chair not far from Spade's. "I knew him as a kid. He's not in trouble, is he?"

Spade said, "I don't know. I'm trying to find him."

Ferris spoke hesitantly: "Can I ask why?"

"You know Gene Colyer?"

"Yes." Ferris hesitated again, then said, "This is in confidence. I've a chain of picture houses through northern California, you know, and a couple of years ago when I had some labor trouble I was told that Colyer was the man to get in touch with to have it straightened out. That's how I happened to meet him."

"Yes," Spade said dryly. "A lot of people happen to meet Gene that way."

"But what's he got to do with Eli?"

"Wants him found. How long since you've seen him?"

"Last Thursday he was here."

"What time did he leave?"

"Midnight—a little after. He came over in the afternoon around half past three. We hadn't seen each other for years. I persuaded him to stay for dinner—he looked pretty seedy—and lent him some money."

"How much?"

"A hundred and fifty—all I had in the house."

"Say where he was going when he left?"

Ferris shook his head. "He said he'd phone me the next day."

"Did he phone you the next day?"

"No."

"And you've known him all his life?"

"Not exactly, but he worked for me fifteen or sixteen years ago when I had a carnival company—Great Eastern and Western Combined Shows—with a partner for a while and then by myself, and I always liked the kid."

"How long before Thursday since you'd seen him?"

"Lord knows," Ferris replied. "I'd lost track of him for years. Then, Wednesday, out of a clear sky, that book came, with no address or anything, just that stuff written in the front, and the next morning he called me up. I was tickled to death to know he was still alive and doing something with himself. So he came over that afternoon and we put in about nine hours straight talking about old times."

"Tell you much about what he'd been doing since then?"

"Just that he'd been knocking around, doing one thing and another, taking the breaks as they came. He didn't complain much; I had to make him take the hundred and fifty."

Spade stood up. "Thanks ever so much, Mr. Ferris. I—"

Ferris interrupted him: "Not at all, and if there's anything I can do, call on me."

Spade looked at his watch. "Can I phone my office to see if anything's turned up?"

"Certainly; there's a phone in the next room, to the right."

Spade said "Thanks" and went out. When he returned he was rolling a cigarette. His face was wooden.

"Any news?" Ferris asked.

"Yes. Colyer's called the job off. He says Haven's body's been found in some bushes on the other side of San Jose, with three bullets in it." He smiled, adding mildly, "He *told* me he might be able to find out something through his connections." ...

Morning sunshine, coming through the curtains that screened Spade's office windows, put two fat, yellow rectangles on the floor and gave everything in the room a yellow tint.

He sat at his desk, staring meditatively at a newspaper. He did not look up when Effie

9

Perine came in from the outer office.

She said, "Mrs. Haven is here."

He raised his head then and said, "That's better. Push her in."

Mrs. Haven came in quickly. Her face was white and she was shivering in spite of her fur coat and the warmth of the day. She came straight to Spade and asked, "Did Gene kill him?"

Spade said, "I don't know."

"I've got to know," she cried.

Spade took her hands. "Here, sit down." He led her to a chair. He asked, "Colyer tell you he'd called the job off?"

She stared at him in amazement. "He what?"

"He left word here last night that your husband had been found and he wouldn't need me any more."

She hung her head and her words were barely audible. "Then he did."

Spade shrugged. "Maybe only an innocent man could've afforded to call it off then, or maybe he was guilty, but had brains enough and nerve enough to—"

She was not listening to him. She was leaning towards him, speaking earnestly: "But, Mr. Spade, you're not going to drop it like that? You're not going to let him stop you?"

While she was speaking his telephone bell rang. He said, "Excuse me," and picked up the receiver. "Yes?... Uh-huh.... So?" He pursed his lips. "I'll let you know." He pushed the telephone aside slowly and faced Mrs. Haven again. "Colyer's outside."

"Does he know I'm here?" she asked quickly.

"Couldn't say." He stood up, pretending he was not watching her closely. "Do you care?"

She pinched her lower lip between her teeth, said "No" hesitantly.

"Fine. I'll have him in."

She raised a hand as if in protest, then let it drop, and her white face was composed. "Whatever you want," she said.

Spade opened the door, said, "Hello, Colyer. Come on in. We were just talking about you."

Colyer nodded and came into the office holding his stick in one hand, his hat in the other. "How are you this morning, Julia? You ought to've phoned me. I'd've driven you back to town."

10

"I—I didn't know what I was doing."

Colyer looked at her for a moment longer, then shifted the focus of his expressionless green eyes to Spade's face. "Well, have you been able to convince her I didn't do it?"

"We hadn't got around to that," Spade said. "I was just trying to find out how much reason there was for suspecting you. Sit down."

Colyer sat down somewhat carefully, asked, "And?"

"And then you arrived."

Colyer nodded gravely. "All right, Spade," he said; "you're hired again to prove to Mrs. Haven that I didn't have anything to do with it."

"Gene!" she exclaimed in a choked voice and held her hands out toward him appealingly. "I don't think you did—I don't want to think you did—but I'm so afraid." She put her hands to her face and began to cry.

Colyer went over to the woman. "Take it easy," he said. "We'll pick it out together."

Spade went into the outer office, shutting the door behind him.

Effie Perine stopped typing a letter.

He grinned at her, said, "Somebody ought to write a book about people sometime— they're peculiar," and went over to the water bottle. "You've got Wally Kellogg's number. Call him up and ask him where I can find Tom Minera."

He returned to the inner office.

Mrs. Haven had stopped crying. She said, "I'm sorry."

Spade said, "It's all right." He looked sidewise at Colyer. "I still got my job?"

"Yes." Colyer cleared his throat. "But if there's nothing special right now, I'd better take Mrs. Haven home."

"O.K., but there's one thing: According to the   Chronicle, you identified him. How come you were down there?"

"I went down when I heard they'd found a body," Colyer replied deliberately. "I told you I had connections. I heard about the body through them."

Spade said, "All right; be seeing you," and opened the door for them.

When the corridor door closed behind them, Effie Perine said, "Minera's at the Buxton on Army Street."

Spade said, "Thanks." He went into the inner office to get his hat. On his way out he said, "If I'm not back in a couple of months tell them to look for my body there." ...

Spade walked down a shabby corridor to a battered green door marked "411." The murmur of voices came through the door, but no words could be distinguished. He stopped listening and knocked.

An obviously disguised male voice asked, "What is it?"

"I want to see Tom. This is Sam Spade."

A pause, then: "Tom ain't here."

Spade put a hand on the knob and shook the frail door. "Come on, open up," he growled.

Presently the door was opened by a thin, dark man of twenty-five or -six who tried to make his beady dark eyes guileless while saying, "I didn't think it was your voice at first." The slackness of his mouth made his chin seem even smaller than it was. His green-striped shirt, open at the neck, was not clean. His gray pants were carefully pressed.

"You've got to be careful these days," Spade said solemnly, and went through the doorway into a room where two men were trying to seem uninterested in his arrival.

One of them leaned against the window sill filing his fingernails. The other was tilted back in a chair with his feet on the edge of a table and a newspaper spread between his hands. They glanced at Spade in unison and went on with their occupations.

Spade said cheerfully, "Always glad to meet any friends of Tom Minera's."

Minera finished shutting the door and said awkwardly, "Uh—yes—Mr. Spade, meet Mr. Conrad and Mr. James."

Conrad, the man at the window, made a vaguely polite gesture with the nail file in his hand. He was a few years older than Minera, of average height, sturdily built, with a thick-featured, dull-eyed face.

James lowered his paper for an instant to look coolly, appraisingly at Spade and say, "How'r'ye, brother?" Then he returned to his reading. He was as sturdily built as Conrad, but taller, and his face had a shrewdness the other's lacked.

"Ah," Spade said, "and friends of the late Eli Haven."

The man at the window jabbed a finger with his nail file, and cursed it bitterly. Minera moistened his lips, and then spoke rapidly, with a whining note in his voice: "But on the level, Spade, we hadn't none of us seen him for a week."

Spade seemed mildly amused by the dark man's manner.

"What do you think he was killed for?"

"All I know is what the paper says: His pockets was all turned inside out and there wasn't as much as a match on him." He drew down the ends of his mouth. "But far as I know he didn't have no dough. He didn't have none Tuesday night."

Spade, speaking softly, said, "I hear he got some Thursday night."

Minera, behind Spade, caught his breath audibly.

James said, "I guess you ought to know. I don't."

"He ever work with you boys?"

James slowly put aside his newspaper and took his feet off the table. His interest in Spade's question seemed great enough, but almost impersonal. "Now what do you mean by that?"

Spade pretended surprise. "But you boys must work at something?"

Minera came around to Spade's side. "Aw, listen, Spade," he said. "This guy Haven was just a guy we knew. We didn't have nothing to do with rubbing him out; we don't know nothing about it. You know, we—"

Three deliberate knocks sounded at the door.

Minera and Conrad looked at James, who nodded, but by then Spade, moving swiftly, had reached the door and was opening it.

Roger Ferris was there.

Spade blinked at Ferris, Ferris at Spade. Then Ferris put out his hand and said, "I *am* glad to see you."

"Come on in," Spade said.

"Look at this, Mr. Spade." Ferris's hand trembled as he took a slightly soiled envelope from his pocket.

Ferris's name and address were typewritten on the envelope. There was no postage stamp on it. Spade took out the enclosure, a narrow slip of cheap white paper, and unfolded it. On it was typewritten:

You had better come to Room No 411 Buxton Hotel on Army St at 5 PM this afternoon on account of Thursday night.

There was no signature.

Spade said, "It's a long time before five o'clock."

"It is," Ferris agreed with emphasis. "I came as soon as I got that. It was Thursday night Eli was at my house."

Minera was jostling Spade, asking, "What is all this?"

Spade held the note up for the dark man to read. He read it and yelled, "Honest, Spade, I don't know nothing about that letter."

"Does anybody?" Spade asked.

Conrad said "No" hastily.

James said, "What letter?"

13

Spade looked dreamily at Ferris for a moment, then said, as if speaking to himself, "Of course, Haven was trying to shake you down."

Ferris's face reddened. "What?"

"Shake-down," Spade repeated patiently; "money, blackmail."

"Look here, Spade," Ferris said earnestly; "you don't really believe what you said? What would he have to blackmail me on?"

"'To good old Buck'"—Spade quoted the dead poet's inscription—"'who knew his colored lights, in memory of them there days.'" He looked somberly at Ferris from beneath slightly raised brows. "What colored lights? What's the circus and carnival slang term for kicking a guy off a train while it's going? Red-lighting. Sure, that's it —red lights. Who'd you red-light, Ferris, that Haven knew about?"

Minera went over to a chair, sat down, put his elbows on his knees, his head between his hands, and stared blankly at the floor. Conrad was breathing as if he had been running.

Spade addressed Ferris: "Well?"

Ferris wiped his face with a handkerchief, put the handkerchief in his pocket, and said simply, "It was a shake-down."

"And you killed him."

Ferris's blue eyes, looking into Spade's yellow-gray ones, were clear and steady, as was his voice. "I did not," he said. "I swear I did not. Let me tell you what happened. He sent me the book, as I told you, and I knew right away what that joke he wrote in the front meant. So the next day, when he phoned me and said he was coming over to talk over old times and to try to borrow some money for old times' sake, I knew what he meant again, and I went down to the bank and drew out ten thousand dollars. You can check that up. It's the Seamen's National."

"I will," Spade said.

"As it turned out, I didn't need that much. He wasn't very big-time and I talked him into taking five thousand. I put the other five back in the bank next day. You can check that up."

"I will," Spade said.

"I told him I wasn't going to stand for any more taps, this five thousand was the first and last. I made him sign a paper saying he'd helped in the—what I'd done—and he signed it. He left sometime around midnight, and that's the last I ever saw of him."

Spade tapped the envelope Ferris had given him. "And how about this note?"

"A messenger boy brought it at noon, and I came right over. Eli had assured me he hadn't said anything to anybody, but I didn't know. I had to face it, whatever it was."

Spade turned to the others, his face wooden. "Well?"

Minera and Conrad looked at James, who made an impatient grimace and said, "Oh, sure, we sent him the letter. Why not? We was friends of Eli's, and we hadn't been able to find him since he went to put the squeeze to this baby, and then he turns up dead, so we kind of like to have the gent come over and explain things."

"You knew about the squeeze?"

"Sure. We was all together when he got the idea."

"How'd he happen to get the idea?" Spade asked.

James spread the fingers of his left hand. "We'd been drinking and talking—you know the way a bunch of guys will, about all they'd seen and done—and he told a yarn about once seeing a guy boot another off a train into a cañon, and he happens to mention the name of the guy that done the booting—Buck Ferris. And somebody says, 'What's this Ferris look like?' Eli tells him what he looked like then, saying he ain't seen him for fifteen years; and whoever it is whistles and says, 'I bet that's the Ferris that owns about half the movie joints in the state. I bet you he'd give something to keep that back trail covered!'

"Well, the idea kind of hit Eli. You could see that. He thought a little while and then he got cagey. He asked what this movie Ferris's first name is, and when the other guy tells him, 'Roger,' he makes out he's disappointed and says, 'No, it ain't him. His first name was Martin.' We all give him the ha-ha and he finally admits he's thinking of seeing the gent, and when he called me up Thursday around noon and says he's throwing a party at Pogey Hecker's that night, it ain't no trouble to figure out what's what."

"What was the name of the gentleman who was red-lighted?"

"He wouldn't say. He shut up tight. You couldn't blame him."

"Uh-huh," Spade agreed.

"Then nothing. He never showed up at Pogey's. We tried to get him on the phone around two o'clock in the morning, but his wife said he hadn't been home, so we stuck around till four or five and then decided he had given us a run-around, and made Pogey charge the bill to him, and beat it. I ain't seen him since—dead or alive."

Spade said mildly. "Maybe. Sure you didn't find Eli later that morning, take him riding, swap him bullets for Ferris's five thou, dump him in the—?"

A sharp double knock sounded on the door.

Spade's face brightened. He went to the door and opened it.

A young man came in. He was very dapper, and very well proportioned. He wore a light topcoat and his hands were in its pockets. Just inside the door he stepped to the right, and stood with his back to the wall. By that time another young man was

15

coming in. He stepped to the left. Though they did not actually look alike, their common dapperness, the similar trimness of their bodies, and their almost identical positions—backs to wall, hands in pockets, cold, bright eyes studying the occupants of the room—gave them, for an instant, the appearance of twins.

Then Gene Colyer came in. He nodded at Spade, but paid no attention to the others in the room, though James said, "Hello, Gene."

"Anything new?" Colyer asked Spade.

Spade nodded. "It seems this gentleman"—he jerked a thumb at Ferris—"was—"

"Any place we can talk?"

"There's a kitchen back here."

Colyer snapped a "Smear anybody that pops" over his shoulder at the two dapper young men and followed Spade into the kitchen. He sat on the one kitchen chair and stared with unblinking green eyes at Spade while Spade told him what he had learned.

When the private detective had finished, the green-eyed man asked, "Well, what do you make of it?"

Spade looked thoughtfully at the other. "You've picked up something. I'd like to know what it is."

Colyer said, "They found the gun in a stream a quarter of a mile from where they found him. It's James's—got the mark on it where it was shot out of his hand once in Vallejo."

"That's nice," Spade said.

"Listen. A kid named Thurber says James comes to him last Wednesday and gets him to tail Haven. Thurber picks him up Thursday afternoon, puts him in at Ferris's, and phones James. James tells him to take a plant on the place and let him know where Haven goes when he leaves, but some nervous woman in the neighborhood puts in a rumble about the kid hanging around, and the cops chase him along about ten o'clock."

Spade pursed his lips and stared thoughtfully at the ceiling.

Colyer's eyes were expressionless, but sweat made his round face shiny, and his voice was hoarse. "Spade," he said, "I'm going to turn him in."

Spade switched his gaze from the ceiling to the protuberant green eyes.

"I've never turned in one of my people before," Colyer said, "but this one goes. Julia's *got* to believe I hadn't anything to do with it if it's one of my people and I turn him in, hasn't she?"

Spade nodded slowly. "I think so."

Colyer suddenly averted his eyes and cleared his throat. When he spoke again it was curtly: "Well, he goes."

Minera, James, and Conrad were seated when Spade and Colyer came out of the kitchen. Ferris was walking the floor. The two dapper young men had not moved.

Colyer went over to James. "Where's your gun, Louis?" he asked.

James moved his right hand a few inches towards his left breast, stopped it, and said, "Oh, I didn't bring it."

With his gloved hand—open—Colyer struck James on the side of the face, knocking him out of his chair.

James straightened up, mumbling, "I didn't mean nothing." He put a hand to the side of his face. "I know I oughtn't've done it, Chief, but when he called up and said he didn't like to go up against Ferris without something and didn't have any of his own, I said, 'All right,' and sent it over to him."

Colyer said, "And you sent Thurber over to him, too."

"We were just kind of interested in seeing if he did go through with it," James mumbled.

"And you couldn't've gone there yourself, or sent somebody else?"

"After Thurber had stirred up the whole neighborhood?"

Colyer turned to Spade. "Want us to help you take them in, or want to call the wagon?"

"We'll do it regular," Spade said, and went to the wall telephone. When he turned away from it his face was wooden, his eyes dreamy. He made a cigarette, lit it, and said to Colyer, "I'm silly enough to think your Louis has got a lot of right answers in that story of his."

James took his hand down from his bruised cheek and stared at Spade with astonished eyes.

Colyer growled, "What's the matter with you?"

"Nothing," Spade said softly, "except I think you're a little too anxious to slam it on him." He blew smoke out. "Why, for instance, should he drop his gun there when it had marks on it that people knew?"

Colyer said, "You think he's got brains."

"If these boys killed him, knew he was dead, why do they wait till the body's found and things are stirred up before they go after Ferris again? What'd they turn his pockets inside out for if they hijacked him? That's a lot of trouble and only done by folks that kill for some other reason and want to make it look like robbery." He shook his head. "You're too anxious to slam it on them. Why should they—?"

17

"That's not the point right now," Colyer said. "The point is, why do you keep saying I'm too anxious to slam it on him?"

Spade shrugged. "Maybe to clear yourself with Julia as soon as possible and as clear as possible, maybe even to clear yourself with the police, and then you've got clients."

Colyer said, "What?"

Spade made a careless gesture with his cigarette. "Ferris," he said blandly. "He killed him, of course."

Colyer's eyelids quivered, though he did not actually blink.

Spade said, "First, he's the last person we know of who saw Eli alive, and that's always a good bet. Second, he's the only person I talked to before Eli's body turned up who cared whether I thought they were holding out on me or not. The rest of you just thought I was hunting for a guy who'd gone away. He knew I was hunting for a man he'd killed, so he had to put himself in the clear. He was even afraid to throw that book away, because it had been sent up by the book store and could be traced, and there might be clerks who'd seen the inscription. Third, he was the only one who thought Eli was just a sweet, clean, lovable boy—for the same reasons. Fourth, that story about a blackmailer showing up at three o'clock in the afternoon, making an easy touch for five grand, and then sticking around till midnight is just silly, no matter how good the booze was. Fifth, the story about the paper Eli signed is still worse, though a forged one could be fixed up easy enough. Sixth, he's got the best reason for anybody we know for wanting Eli dead."

Colyer nodded slowly. "Still—"

"Still nothing," Spade said. "Maybe he did the ten-thousand-out-five-thousand-back trick with his bank, but that was easy. Then he got this feeble-minded blackmailer in his house, stalled him along until the servants had gone to bed, took the borrowed gun away from him, shoved him downstairs into his car, took him for a ride—maybe took him already dead, maybe shot him down there by the bushes—frisked him clean to make identification harder and to make it look like robbery, tossed the gun in the water, and came home—"

He broke off to listen to the sound of a siren in the street. He looked then, for the first time since he had begun to talk, at Ferris.

Ferris's face was ghastly white, but he held his eyes steady.

Spade said, "I've got a hunch, Ferris, that we're going to find out about that red-lighting job, too. You told me you had your carnival company with a partner for a while when Eli was working for you, and then by yourself. We oughtn't to have a lot of trouble finding out about your partner—whether he disappeared, or died a natural death, or is still alive."

Ferris had lost some of his erectness. He wet his lips and said, "I want to see my lawyer. I don't want to talk till I've seen my lawyer."

Spade said, "It's all right with me. You're up against it, but I don't like blackmailers myself. I think Eli wrote a good epitaph for them in that book back there—'Too many have lived.'"

THEY CAN ONLY HANG YOU ONCE

Samuel Spade said: "My name is Ronald Ames. I want to see Mr. Binnett—Mr. Timothy Binnett."

"Mr. Binnett is resting now, sir," the butler replied hesitantly.

"Will you find out when I can see him? It's important." Spade cleared his throat. "I'm —uh—just back from Australia, and it's about some of his properties there."

The butler turned on his heel while saying "I'll see, sir," and was going up the front stairs before he had finished speaking.

Spade made and lit a cigarette.

The butler came downstairs again. "I'm sorry; he can't be disturbed now, but Mr. Wallace Binnett—Mr. Timothy's nephew—will see you."

Spade said, "Thanks," and followed the butler upstairs.

Wallace Binnett was a slender, handsome, dark man of about Spade's age—thirty-eight—who rose smiling from a brocaded chair, said, "How do you do, Mr. Ames?" waved his hand at another chair, and sat down again. "You're from Australia?"

"Got in this morning."

"You're a business associate of Uncle Tim's?"

Spade smiled and shook his head. "Hardly that, but I've some information I think he ought to have—quick."

Wallace Binnett looked thoughtfully at the floor, then up at Spade. "I'll do my best to persuade him to see you, Mr. Ames, but, frankly, I don't know."

Spade seemed mildly surprised. "Why?"

Binnett shrugged. "He's peculiar sometimes. Understand, his mind seems perfectly all right, but he has the testiness and eccentricity of an old man in ill health and—well—at times he can be difficult."

Spade asked slowly: "He's already refused to see me?"

"Yes."

Spade rose from his chair. His blond satan's face was expressionless.

19

Binnett raised a hand quickly. "Wait, wait," he said. "I'll do what I can to make him change his mind. Perhaps if—" His dark eyes suddenly became wary. "You're not simply trying to sell him something, are you?"

"No."

The wary gleam went out of Binnett's eyes. "Well, then, I think I can—"

A young woman came in crying angrily, "Wally, that old fool has—" She broke off with a hand to her breast when she saw Spade.

Spade and Binnett had risen together. Binnett said suavely: "Joyce, this is Mr. Ames. My sister-in-law, Joyce Court."

Spade bowed.

Joyce Court uttered a short, embarrassed laugh and said: "Please excuse my whirlwind entrance." She was a tall, blue-eyed, dark woman of twenty-four or -five with good shoulders and a strong, slim body. Her features made up in warmth what they lacked in regularity. She wore wide-legged blue satin pajamas.

Binnett smiled good-naturedly at her and asked: "Now what's all the excitement?"

Anger darkened her eyes again and she started to speak. Then she looked at Spade and said: "But we shouldn't bore Mr. Ames with our stupid domestic affairs. If—" She hesitated.

Spade bowed again. "Sure," he said, "certainly."

"I won't be a minute," Binnett promised, and left the room with her.

Spade went to the open doorway through which they had vanished and, standing just inside, listened. Their footsteps became inaudible. Nothing else could be heard. Spade was standing there—his yellow-gray eyes dreamy—when he heard the scream. It was a woman's scream, high and shrill with terror. Spade was through the doorway when he heard the shot. It was a pistol shot, magnified, reverberated by walls and ceilings.

Twenty feet from the doorway Spade found a staircase, and went up it three steps at a time. He turned to the left. Halfway down the hallway a woman lay on her back on the floor.

Wallace Binnett knelt beside her, fondling one of her hands desperately, crying in a low, beseeching voice: "Darling, Molly, darling!"

Joyce Court stood behind him and wrung her hands while tears streaked her cheeks.

The woman on the floor resembled Joyce Court but was older, and her face had a hardness the younger one's had not.

"She's dead, she's been killed," Wallace Binnett said incredulously, raising his white face towards Spade. When Binnett moved his head Spade could see the round hole in

20

the woman's tan dress over her heart and the dark stain which was rapidly spreading below it.

Spade touched Joyce Court's arm. "Police, emergency hospital—phone," he said. As she ran towards the stairs he addressed Wallace Binnett: "Who did—"

A voice groaned feebly behind Spade.

He turned swiftly. Through an open doorway he could see an old man in white pajamas lying sprawled across a rumpled bed. His head, a shoulder, an arm dangled over the edge of the bed. His other hand held his throat tightly. He groaned again and his eyelids twitched, but did not open.

Spade lifted the old man's head and shoulders and put them up on the pillows. The old man groaned again and took his hand from his throat. His throat was red with half a dozen bruises. He was a gaunt man with a seamed face that probably exaggerated his age.

A glass of water was on a table beside the bed. Spade put water on the old man's face and, when the old man's eyes twitched again, leaned down and growled softly: "Who did it?"

The twitching eyelids went up far enough to show a narrow strip of bloodshot gray eyes. The old man spoke painfully, putting a hand to his throat again: "A man—he—" He coughed.

Spade made an impatient grimace. His lips almost touched the old man's ear. "Where'd he go?" His voice was urgent.

A gaunt hand moved weakly to indicate the rear of the house and fell back on the bed.

The butler and two frightened female servants had joined Wallace Binnett beside the dead woman in the hallway.

"Who did it?" Spade asked them.

They stared at him blankly.

"Somebody look after the old man," he growled, and went down the hallway.

At the end of the hallway was a rear staircase. He descended two flights and went through a pantry into the kitchen. He saw nobody. The kitchen door was shut but, when he tried it, not locked. He crossed a narrow back yard to a gate that was shut, not locked. He opened the gate. There was nobody in the narrow alley behind it.

He sighed, shut the gate, and returned to the house.

Spade sat comfortably slack in a deep leather chair in a room that ran across the front second story of Wallace Binnett's house. There were shelves of books and the lights were on. The window showed outer darkness weakly diluted by a distant street lamp. Facing Spade, Detective Sergeant Polhaus—a big, carelessly shaven, florid man in dark clothes that needed pressing—was sprawled in another leather chair; Lieutenant Dundy—smaller, compactly built, square-faced—stood with legs apart, head thrust a little forward, in the center of the room.

Spade was saying: "... and the doctor would only let me talk to the old man a couple of minutes. We can try it again when he's rested a little, but it doesn't look like he knows much. He was catching a nap and he woke up with somebody's hands on his throat dragging him around the bed. The best he got was a one-eyed look at the fellow choking him. A big fellow, he says, with a soft hat pulled down over his eyes, dark, needing a shave. Sounds like Tom." Spade nodded at Polhaus.

The detective sergeant chuckled, but Dundy said, "Go on," curtly.

Spade grinned and went on: "He's pretty far gone when he hears Mrs. Binnett scream at the door. The hands go away from his throat and he hears the shot and just before passing out he gets a flash of the big fellow heading for the rear of the house and Mrs. Binnett tumbling down on the hall floor. He says he never saw the big fellow before."

"What size gun was it?" Dundy asked.

"Thirty-eight. Well, nobody in the house is much more help. Wallace and his sister-in-law, Joyce, were in her room, so they say, and didn't see anything but the dead woman when they ran out, though they think they heard something that could've been somebody running downstairs—the back stairs.

"The butler—his name's Jarboe—was in here when he heard the scream and shot, so he says. Irene Kelly, the maid, was down on the ground floor, so she says. The cook, Margaret Finn, was in her room—third floor back—and didn't even hear anything, so she says. She's deaf as a post, so everybody else says. The back door and gate were unlocked, but are supposed to be kept locked, so everybody says. Nobody says they were in or around the kitchen or yard at the time." Spade spread his hands in a gesture of finality. "That's the crop."

Dundy shook his head. "Not exactly," he said. "How come you were here?"

Spade's face brightened. "Maybe my client killed her," he said. "He's Wallace's cousin, Ira Binnett. Know him?"

Dundy shook his head. His blue eyes were hard and suspicious.

"He's a San Francisco lawyer," Spade said, "respectable and all that. A couple of days ago he came to me with a story about his uncle Timothy, a miserly old skinflint, lousy with money and pretty well broken up by hard living. He was the black sheep of the family. None of them had heard of him for years. But six or eight months ago he showed up in pretty bad shape every way except financially—he seems to have taken a lot of money out of Australia—wanting to spend his last days with his only living relatives, his nephews Wallace and Ira.

"That was all right with them. 'Only living relatives' meant 'only heirs' in their language. But by and by the nephews began to think it was better to be an heir than to be one of a couple of heirs—twice as good, in fact—and started fiddling for the inside track with the old man. At least, that's what Ira told me about Wallace, and I wouldn't be surprised if Wallace would say the same thing about Ira, though Wallace seems to be the harder up of the two. Anyhow, the nephews fell out, and then Uncle Tim, who had been staying at Ira's, came over here. That was a couple of months ago, and Ira hasn't seen Uncle Tim since, and hasn't been able to get in touch with him by phone or mail.

"That's what he wanted a private detective about. He didn't think Uncle Tim would come to any harm here—oh, no, he went to a lot of trouble to make that clear—but he thought maybe undue pressure was being brought to bear on the old boy, or he was being hornswoggled somehow, and at least being told lies about his loving nephew Ira. He wanted to know what was what. I waited until today, when a boat from Australia docked, and came up here as a Mr. Ames with some important information for Uncle Tim about his properties down there. All I wanted was fifteen minutes alone with him." Spade frowned thoughtfully. "Well, I didn't get them. Wallace told me the old man refused to see me. I don't know."

Suspicion had deepened in Dundy's cold blue eyes. "And where is this Ira Binnett now?" he asked.

Spade's yellow-gray eyes were as guileless as his voice. "I wish I knew. I phoned his house and office and left word for him to come right over, but I'm afraid—"

Knuckles knocked sharply twice on the other side of the room's one door. The three men in the room turned to face the door.

Dundy called, "Come in."

The door was opened by a sunburned blond policeman whose left hand held the right wrist of a plump man of forty or forty-five in well-fitting gray clothes. The policeman pushed the plump man into the room. "Found him monkeying with the kitchen door," he said.

Spade looked up and said: "Ah!" His tone expressed satisfaction. "Mr. Ira Binnett, Lieutenant Dundy, Sergeant Polhaus."

Ira Binnett said rapidly: "Mr. Spade, will you tell this man that—"

Dundy addressed the policeman: "All right. Good work. You can leave him."

The policeman moved a hand vaguely towards his cap and went away.

Dundy glowered at Ira Binnett and demanded, "Well?"

Binnett looked from Dundy to Spade. "Has something—"

Spade said: "Better tell him why you were at the back door instead of the front."

Ira Binnett suddenly blushed. He cleared his throat in embarrassment. He said: "I—

uh—I should explain. It wasn't my fault, of course, but when Jarboe—he's the butler —phoned me that Uncle Tim wanted to see me, he told me he'd leave the kitchen door unlocked, so Wallace wouldn't have to know I'd—"

"What'd he want to see you about?" Dundy asked.

"I don't know. He didn't say. He said it was very important."

"Didn't you get my message?" Spade asked.

Ira Binnett's eyes widened. "No. What was it? Has anything happened? What is—"

Spade was moving toward the door. "Go ahead," he said to Dundy. "I'll be right back."

He shut the door carefully behind him and went up to the third floor.

The butler Jarboe was on his knees at Timothy Binnett's door with an eye to the keyhole. On the floor beside him was a tray holding an egg in an egg-cup, toast, a pot of coffee, china, silver, and a napkin.

Spade said: "Your toast's going to get cold."

Jarboe, scrambling to his feet, almost upsetting the coffeepot in his haste, his face red and sheepish, stammered: "I—er—beg your pardon, sir. I wanted to make sure Mr. Timothy was awake before I took this in." He picked up the tray. "I didn't want to disturb his rest if—"

Spade, who had reached the door, said, "Sure, sure," and bent over to put his eye to the keyhole. When he straightened up he said in a mildly complaining tone: "You can't see the bed—only a chair and part of the window."

The butler replied quickly: "Yes, sir, I found that out."

Spade laughed.

The butler coughed, seemed about to say something, but did not. He hesitated, then knocked lightly on the door.

A tired voice said, "Come in."

Spade asked quickly in a low voice: "Where's Miss Court?"

"In her room, I think, sir, the second door on the left," the butler said.

The tired voice inside the room said petulantly: "Well, come on in."

The butler opened the door and went in. Through the door, before the butler shut it, Spade caught a glimpse of Timothy Binnett propped up on pillows in his bed.

Spade went to the second door on the left and knocked. The door was opened almost immediately by Joyce Court. She stood in the doorway, not smiling, not speaking.

He said: "Miss Court, when you came into the room where I was with your brother-

24

in-law you said, 'Wally, that old fool has—' Meaning Timothy?"

She stared at Spade for a moment. Then: "Yes."

"Mind telling me what the rest of the sentence would have been?"

She said slowly: "I don't know who you really are or why you ask, but I don't mind telling you. It would have been 'sent for Ira.' Jarboe had just told me."

"Thanks."

She shut the door before he had turned away.

He returned to Timothy Binnett's door and knocked on it.

"Who is it now?" the old man's voice demanded.

Spade opened the door. The old man was sitting up in bed.

Spade said: "This Jarboe was peeping through your keyhole a few minutes ago," and returned to the library.

Ira Binnett, seated in the chair Spade had occupied, was saying to Dundy and Polhaus: "And Wallace got caught in the crash, like most of us, but he seems to have juggled accounts trying to save himself. He was expelled from the Stock Exchange."

Dundy waved a hand to indicate the room and its furnishings. "Pretty classy layout for a man that's busted."

"His wife has some money," Ira Binnett said, "and he always lived beyond his means."

Dundy scowled at Binnett. "And you really think he and his missus weren't on good terms?"

"I don't think it," Binnett replied evenly. "I know it."

Dundy nodded. "And you know he's got a yen for the sister-in-law, this Court?"

"I don't know that. But I've heard plenty of gossip to the same effect."

Dundy made a growling noise in his throat, then asked sharply: "How does the old man's will read?"

"I don't know. I don't know whether he's made one." He addressed Spade, now earnestly: "I've told everything I know, every single thing."

Dundy said, "It's not enough." He jerked a thumb at the door. "Show him where to wait, Tom, and let's have the widower in again."

Big Polhaus said, "Right," went out with Ira Binnett, and returned with Wallace Binnett, whose face was hard and pale.

Dundy asked: "Has your uncle made a will?"

"I don't know," Binnett replied.

Spade put the next question, softly: "Did your wife?"

Binnett's mouth tightened in a mirthless smile. He spoke deliberately: "I'm going to say some things I'd rather not have to say. My wife, properly, had no money. When I got into financial trouble some time ago I made some property over to her, to save it. She turned it into money without my knowing about it till afterwards. She paid our bills—our living expenses—out of it, but she refused to return it to me and she assured me that in no event—whether she lived or died or we stayed together or were divorced—would I ever be able to get hold of a penny of it. I believed her, and still do."

"You wanted a divorce?" Dundy asked.

"Yes."

"Why?"

"It wasn't a happy marriage."

"Joyce Court?"

Binnett's face flushed. He said stiffly: "I admire Joyce Court tremendously, but I'd've wanted a divorce anyway."

Spade said: "And you're sure—still absolutely sure—you don't know anybody who fits your uncle's description of the man who choked him?"

"Absolutely sure."

The sound of the doorbell ringing came faintly into the room.

Dundy said sourly, "That'll do."

Binnett went out.

Polhaus said: "That guy's as wrong as they make them. And—"

From below came the heavy report of a pistol fired indoors.

The lights went out.

In darkness the three detectives collided with one another going through the doorway into the dark hall. Spade reached the stairs first. There was a clatter of footsteps below him, but nothing could be seen until he reached a bend in the stairs. Then enough light came from the street through the open front door to show the dark figure of a man standing with his back to the open door.

A flashlight clicked in Dundy's hand—he was at Spade's heels—and threw a glaring white beam of light on the man's face. He was Ira Binnett. He blinked in the light and pointed at something on the floor in front of him.

Dundy turned the beam of his light down on the floor. Jarboe lay there on his face,

26

bleeding from a bullet hole in the back of his head.

Spade grunted softly.

Tom Polhaus came blundering down the stairs, Wallace Binnett close behind him. Joyce Court's frightened voice came from farther up: "Oh, what's happened? Wally, what's happened?"

"Where's the light switch?" Dundy barked.

"Inside the cellar door, under these stairs," Wallace Binnett said. "What is it?"

Polhaus pushed past Binnett towards the cellar door.

Spade made an inarticulate sound in his throat and, pushing Wallace Binnett aside, sprang up the stairs. He brushed past Joyce Court and went on, heedless of her startled scream. He was half way up the stairs to the third floor when the pistol went off up there.

He ran to Timothy Binnett's door. The door was open. He went in.

Something hard and angular struck him above his right ear, knocking him across the room, bringing him down on one knee. Something thumped and clattered on the floor just outside the door.

The lights came on.

On the floor, in the center of the room, Timothy Binnett lay on his back bleeding from a bullet wound in his left forearm. His pajama jacket was torn. His eyes were shut.

Spade stood up and put a hand to his head. He scowled at the old man on the floor, at the room, at the black automatic pistol lying on the hallway floor. He said: "Come on, you old cutthroat. Get up and sit on a chair and I'll see if I can stop that bleeding till the doctor gets here."

The man on the floor did not move.

There were footsteps in the hallway and Dundy came in, followed by the two younger Binnetts. Dundy's face was dark and furious. "Kitchen door wide open," he said in a choked voice. "They run in and out like—"

"Forget it," Spade said. "Uncle Tim is our meat." He paid no attention to Wallace Binnett's gasp, to the incredulous looks on Dundy's and Ira Binnett's faces. "Come on, get up," he said to the old man on the floor, "and tell us what it was the butler saw when he peeped through the keyhole."

The old man did not stir.

"He killed the butler because I told him the butler had peeped," Spade explained to Dundy. "I peeped, too, but didn't see anything except that chair and the window, though we'd made enough racket by then to scare him back to bed. Suppose you take

27

the chair apart while I go over the window." He went to the window and began to examine it carefully. He shook his head, put a hand out behind him, and said: "Give me the flashlight."

Dundy put the flashlight in his hand.

Spade raised the window and leaned out, turning the light on the outside of the building. Presently he grunted and put his other hand out, tugging at a brick a little below the sill. Presently the brick came loose. He put it on the window sill and stuck his hand into the hole its removal had made. Out of the opening, one at a time, he brought an empty black pistol holster, a partially filled box of cartridges, and an unsealed manila envelope.

Holding these things in his hands, he turned to face the others. Joyce Court came in with a basin of water and a roll of gauze and knelt beside Timothy Binnett. Spade put the holster and cartridges on a table and opened the manila envelope. Inside were two sheets of paper, covered on both sides with boldly penciled writing. Spade read a paragraph to himself, suddenly laughed, and began at the beginning again, reading aloud:

"'I, Timothy Kieran Binnett, being sound of mind and body, do declare this to be my last will and testament. To my dear nephews, Ira Binnett and Wallace Bourke Binnett, in recognition of the loving kindness with which they have received me into their homes and attended my declining years, I give and bequeath, share and share alike, all my worldly possessions of whatever kind, to wit, my carcass and the clothes I stand in.

"'I bequeath them, furthermore, the expense of my funeral and these memories: First, the memory of their credulity in believing that the fifteen years I spent in Sing Sing were spent in Australia; second, the memory of their optimism in supposing that those fifteen years had brought me great wealth, and that if I lived on them, borrowed from them, and never spent any of my own money, it was because I was a miser whose hoard they would inherit; and not because I had no money except what I shook them down for; third, for their hopefulness in thinking that I would leave either of them anything if I had it; and, lastly because their painful lack of any decent sense of humor will keep them from ever seeing how funny this has all been. Signed and sealed this—'"

Spade looked up to say: "There is no date, but it's signed Timothy Kieran Binnett with flourishes."

Ira Binnett was purple with anger, Wallace's face was ghastly in its pallor and his whole body was trembling. Joyce Court had stopped working on Timothy Binnett's arm.

The old man sat up and opened his eyes. He looked at his nephews and began to laugh. There was in his laughter neither hysteria nor madness: it was sane, hearty laughter, and subsided slowly.

Spade said: "All right, now you've had your fun. Let's talk about the killings."

"I know nothing more about the first one than I've told you," the old man said, "and this one's not a killing, since I'm only—"

Wallace Binnett, still trembling violently, said painfully through his teeth: "That's a lie. You killed Molly. Joyce and I came out of her room when we heard Molly scream, and heard the shot and saw her fall out of your room, and nobody came out afterwards."

The old man said calmly: "Well, I'll tell you: it was an accident. They told me there was a fellow from Australia here to see me about some of my properties there. I knew there was something funny about that somewhere"—he grinned—"not ever having been there. I didn't know whether one of my dear nephews was getting suspicious and putting up a game on me or what, but I knew that if Wally wasn't in on it he'd certainly try to pump the gentleman from Australia about me and maybe I'd lose one of my free boarding houses." He chuckled.

"So I figured I'd get in touch with Ira so I could go back to his house if things worked out bad here, and I'd try to get rid of this Australian. Wally's always thought I'm half-cracked"—he leered at his nephew—"and's afraid they'll lug me off to a madhouse before I could make a will in his favor, or they'll break it if I do. You see, he's got a pretty bad reputation, what with that Stock Exchange trouble and all, and he knows no court would appoint him to handle my affairs if I went screwy—not as long as I've got another nephew"—he turned his leer on Ira—"who's a respectable lawyer. So now I know that rather than have me kick up a row that might wind me up in the madhouse, he'll chase this visitor, and I put on a show for Molly, who happened to be the nearest one to hand. She took it too seriously, though.

"I had a gun and I did a lot of raving about being spied on by my enemies in Australia and that I was going down and shoot this fellow. But she got too excited and tried to take the gun away from me, and the first thing I knew it had gone off, and I had to make these marks on my neck and think up that story about the big dark man." He looked contemptuously at Wallace. "I didn't know he was covering me up. Little as I thought of him, I never thought he'd be low enough to cover up his wife's murderer—even if he didn't like her—just for the sake of money."

Spade said: "Never mind that. Now about the butler?"

"I don't know anything about the butler," the old man replied, looking at Spade with steady eyes.

Spade said: "You had to kill him quick, before he had time to do or say anything. So you slip down the back stairs, open the kitchen door to fool people, go to the front door, ring the bell, shut the door, and hide in the shadow of the cellar door under the front steps. When Jarboe answered the doorbell you shot him—the hole was in the back of his head—pulled the light switch, just inside the cellar door, and ducked up the back stairs in the dark and shot yourself carefully in the arm. I got up there too

29

soon for you; so you smacked me with the gun, chucked it through the door, and spread yourself on the floor while I was shaking pinwheels out of my noodle."

The old man sniffed again. "You're just—"

"Stop it," Spade said patiently. "Don't let's argue. The first killing was an accident— all right. The second couldn't be. And it ought to be easy to show that both bullets, and the one in your arm, were fired from the same gun. What difference does it make which killing we can prove first-degree murder on? They can only hang you once." He smiled pleasantly. "And they will."

A MAN CALLED SPADE

Samuel Spade put his telephone aside and looked at his watch. It was not quite four o'clock. He called, "Yoo-hoo!"

Effie Perine came in from the outer office. She was eating a piece of chocolate cake.

"Tell Sid Wise I won't be able to keep that date this afternoon," he said.

She put the last of the cake into her mouth and licked the tips of forefinger and thumb. "That's the third time this week."

When he smiled, the v's of his chin, mouth, and brows grew longer. "I know, but I've got to go out and save a life." He nodded at the telephone. "Somebody's scaring Max Bliss."

She laughed. "Probably somebody named John D. Conscience."

He looked up at her from the cigarette he had begun to make. "Know anything I ought to know about him?"

"Nothing you don't know. I was just thinking about the time he let his brother go to San Quentin."

Spade shrugged. "That's not the worst thing he's done." He lit his cigarette, stood up, and reached for his hat. "But he's all right now. All Samuel Spade clients are honest, God-fearing folk. If I'm not back at closing time just run along."

He went to a tall apartment building on Nob Hill, pressed a button set in the frame of a door marked   10K. The door was opened immediately by a burly dark man in wrinkled dark clothes. He was nearly bald and carried a gray hat in one hand.

The burly man said, "Hello, Sam." He smiled, but his small eyes lost none of their shrewdness. "What are you doing here?"

Spade said, "Hello, Tom." His face was wooden, his voice expressionless. "Bliss in?"

"Is he!" Tom pulled down the corners of his thick-lipped mouth. "You don't have to worry about that."

Spade's brows came together. "Well?"

A man appeared in the vestibule behind Tom. He was smaller than either Spade or Tom, but compactly built. He had a ruddy, square face and a close-trimmed, grizzled mustache. His clothes were neat. He wore a black bowler perched on the back of his head.

Spade addressed this man over Tom's shoulder: "Hello, Dundy."

Dundy nodded briefly and came to the door. His blue eyes were hard and prying.

"What is it?" he asked Tom.

"B-l-i-s-s, M-a-x," Spade spelled patiently. "I want to see him. He wants to see me. Catch on?"

Tom laughed. Dundy did not. Tom said, "Only one of you gets your wish." Then he glanced sidewise at Dundy and abruptly stopped laughing. He seemed uncomfortable.

Spade scowled. "All right," he demanded irritably; "is he dead or has he killed somebody?"

Dundy thrust his square face up at Spade and seemed to push his words out with his lower lip. "What makes you think either?"

Spade said, "Oh, sure! I come calling on Mr. Bliss and I'm stopped at the door by a couple of men from the police Homicide Detail, and I'm supposed to think I'm just interrupting a game of rummy."

"Aw, stop it, Sam," Tom grumbled, looking at neither Spade nor Dundy. "He's dead."

"Killed?"

Tom wagged his head slowly up and down. He looked at Spade now. "What've you got on it?"

Spade replied in a deliberate monotone, "He called me up this afternoon—say at five minutes to four—I looked at my watch after he hung up and there was still a minute or so to go—and said somebody was after his scalp. He wanted me to come over. It seemed real enough to him—it was up in his neck all right." He made a small gesture with one hand. "Well, here I am."

"Didn't say who or how?" Dundy asked.

Spade shook his head. "No. Just somebody had offered to kill him and he believed them, and would I come over right away."

"Didn't he—?" Dundy began quickly.

"He didn't say anything else," Spade said. "Don't you people tell me anything?"

31

Dundy said curtly, "Come in and take a look at him."

Tom said, "It's a sight."

They went across the vestibule and through a door into a green and rose living-room.

A man near the door stopped sprinkling white powder on the end of a glass-covered small table to say, "Hello, Sam."

Spade nodded, said, "How are you, Phels?" and then nodded at the two men who stood talking by a window.

The dead man lay with his mouth open. Some of his clothes had been taken off. His throat was puffy and dark. The end of his tongue showing in a corner of his mouth was bluish, swollen. On his bare chest, over the heart, a five-pointed star had been outlined in black ink and in the center of it a T.

Spade looked down at the dead man and stood for a moment silently studying him. Then he asked, "He was found like that?"

"About," Tom said. "We moved him around a little." He jerked a thumb at the shirt, undershirt, vest, and coat lying on a table. "They were spread over the floor."

Spade rubbed his chin. His yellow-gray eyes were dreamy. "When?"

Tom said, "We got it at four-twenty. His daughter gave it to us." He moved his head to indicate a closed door. "You'll see her."

"Know anything?"

"Heaven knows," Tom said wearily. "She's been kind of hard to get along with so far." He turned to Dundy. "Want to try her again now?"

Dundy nodded, then spoke to one of the men at the window. "Start sifting his papers, Mack. He's supposed to've been threatened."

Mack said, "Right." He pulled his hat down over his eyes and walked towards a green secrétaire in the far end of the room.

A man came in from the corridor, a heavy man of fifty with a deeply lined, grayish face under a broad-brimmed black hat. He said, "Hello, Sam," and then told Dundy, "He had company around half past two, stayed just about an hour. A big blond man in brown, maybe forty or forty-five. Didn't send his name up. I got it from the Filipino in the elevator that rode him both ways."

"Sure it was only an hour?" Dundy asked.

The gray-faced man shook his head. "But he's sure it wasn't more than half past three when he left. He says the afternoon papers came in then, and this man had ridden down with him before they came." He pushed his hat back to scratch his head, then pointed a thick finger at the design inked on the dead man's breast and asked somewhat plaintively, "What the deuce do you suppose that thing is?"

32

Nobody replied. Dundy asked, "Can the elevator boy identify him?"

"He says he could, but that ain't always the same thing. Says he never saw him before." He stopped looking at the dead man. "The girl's getting me a list of his phone calls. How you been, Sam?"

Spade said he had been all right. Then he said slowly, "His brother's big and blond and maybe forty or forty-five."

Dundy's blue eyes were hard and bright. "So what?" he asked.

"You remember the Graystone Loan swindle. They were both in it, but Max eased the load over on Theodore and it turned out to be one to fourteen years in San Quentin."

Dundy was slowly wagging his head up and down. "I remember now. Where is he?"

Spade shrugged and began to make a cigarette.

Dundy nudged Tom with an elbow. "Find out."

Tom said, "Sure, but if he was out of here at half past three and this fellow was still alive at five to four—"

"And he broke his leg so he couldn't duck back in," the gray-faced man said jovially.

"Find out," Dundy repeated.

Tom said, "Sure, sure," and went to the telephone.

Dundy addressed the gray-faced man: "Check up on the newspapers; see what time they were actually delivered this afternoon."

The gray-faced man nodded and left the room.

The man who had been searching the secrétaire said, "Uh-huh," and turned around holding an envelope in one hand, a sheet of paper in the other.

Dundy held out his hand. "Something?"

The man said, "Uh-huh," again and gave Dundy the sheet of paper.

Spade was looking over Dundy's shoulder.

It was a small sheet of common white paper bearing a penciled message in neat, undistinguished handwriting:

When this reaches you I will be too close for you to escape—this time. We will balance our accounts—for good.

The signature was a five-pointed star enclosing a T, the design on the dead man's left breast.

Dundy held out his hand again and was given the envelope. Its stamp was French. The address was typewritten:

MAX BLISS, ESQ.AMSTERDAM
APARTMENTS,SAN FRANCISCO, CALIF.U. S. A.

"Postmarked Paris," he said, "the second of the month." He counted swiftly on his fingers. "That would get it here today, all right." He folded the message slowly, put it in the envelope, put the envelope in his coat pocket. "Keep digging," he told the man who had found the message.

The man nodded and returned to the secrétaire.

Dundy looked at Spade. "What do you think of it?"

Spade's brown cigarette wagged up and down with the words. "I don't like it. I don't like any of it."

Tom put down the telephone. "He got out the fifteenth of last month," he said. "I got them trying to locate him."

Spade went to the telephone, called a number, and asked for Mr. Darrell. Then: "Hello, Harry, this is Sam Spade.... Fine. How's Lil?... Yes.... Listen, Harry, what does a five-pointed star with a capital T in the middle mean?... What? How do you spell it?... Yes, I see.... And if you found it on a body?... Neither do I.... Yes, and thanks. I'll tell you about it when I see you.... Yes, give me a ring.... Thanks.... 'By."

Dundy and Tom were watching him closely when he turned from the telephone. He said, "That's a fellow who knows things sometimes. He says it's a pentagram with a Greek tau—t-a-u—in the middle; a sign magicians used to use. Maybe Rosicrucians still do."

"What's a Rosicrucian?" Tom asked.

"It could be Theodore's first initial, too," Dundy said.

Spade moved his shoulders, said carelessly, "Yes, but if he wanted to autograph the job it'd been just as easy for him to sign his name."

He then went on more thoughtfully, "There are Rosicrucians at both San Jose and Point Loma. I don't go much for this, but maybe we ought to look them up."

Dundy nodded.

Spade looked at the dead man's clothes on the table. "Anything in his pockets?"

"Only what you'd expect to find," Dundy replied. "It's on the table there."

Spade went to the table and looked down at the little pile of watch and chain, keys, wallet, address book, money, gold pencil, handkerchief, and spectacle case beside the clothing. He did not touch them, but slowly picked up, one at a time, the dead man's shirt, undershirt, vest, and coat. A blue necktie lay on the table beneath them. He scowled irritably at it. "It hasn't been worn," he complained.

Dundy, Tom, and the coroner's deputy, who had stood silent all this while by the

34

window—he was a small man with a slim, dark, intelligent face—came together to stare down at the unwrinkled blue silk.

Tom groaned miserably. Dundy cursed under his breath. Spade lifted the necktie to look at its back. The label was a London haberdasher's.

Spade said cheerfully, "Swell. San Francisco, Point Loma, San Jose, Paris, London."

Dundy glowered at him.

The gray-faced man came in. "The papers got here at three-thirty, all right," he said. His eyes widened a little. "What's up?" As he crossed the room towards them he said, "I can't find anybody that saw Blondy sneak back in here again." He looked uncomprehendingly at the necktie until Tom growled, "It's brand-new"; then he whistled softly.

Dundy turned to Spade. "The deuce with all this," he said bitterly. "He's got a brother with reasons for not liking him. The brother just got out of stir. Somebody who looks like his brother left here at half past three. Twenty-five minutes later he phoned you he'd been threatened. Less than half an hour after that his daughter came in and found him dead—strangled." He poked a finger at the small, dark-faced man's chest. "Right?"

"Strangled," the dark-faced man said precisely, "by a man. The hands were large."

"O. K." Dundy turned to Spade again. "We find a threatening letter. Maybe that's what he was telling you about, maybe it was something his brother said to him. Don't let's guess. Let's stick to what we know. We know he—"

The man at the secrétaire turned around and said, "Got another one." His mien was somewhat smug.

The eyes with which the five men at the table looked at him were identically cold, unsympathetic.

He, nowise disturbed by their hostility, read aloud:

"Dear Bliss:

"I am writing this to tell you for the last time that I want my money back, and I want it back by the first of the month, all of it. If I don't get it I am going to do something about it, and you ought to be able to guess what I mean. And don't think I am kidding.

"Yours truly,
"Daniel Talbot."

He grinned. "That's another T for you." He picked up an envelope. "Postmarked San Diego, the twenty-fifth of last month." He grinned again. "And that's another city for you."

35

Spade shook his head. "Point Loma's down that way," he said.

He went over with Dundy to look at the letter. It was written in blue ink on white stationery of good quality, as was the address on the envelope, in a cramped, angular handwriting that seemed to have nothing in common with that of the penciled letter.

Spade said ironically, "Now we're getting somewhere."

Dundy made an impatient gesture. "Let's stick to what we know," he growled.

"Sure," Spade agreed. "What is it?"

There was no reply.

Spade took tobacco and cigarette papers from his pocket. "Didn't somebody say something about talking to a daughter?" he asked.

"We'll talk to her." Dundy turned on his heel, then suddenly frowned at the dead man on the floor. He jerked a thumb at the small, dark-faced man. "Through with it?"

"I'm through."

Dundy addressed Tom curtly: "Get rid of it." He addressed the gray-faced man: "I want to see both elevator boys when I'm finished with the girl."

He went to the closed door Tom had pointed out to Spade and knocked on it.

A slightly harsh female voice within asked, "What is it?"

"Lieutenant Dundy. I want to talk to Miss Bliss."

There was a pause; then the voice said, "Come in."

Dundy opened the door and Spade followed him into a black, gray, and silver room, where a big-boned and ugly middle-aged woman in black dress and white apron sat beside a bed on which a girl lay.

The girl lay, elbow on pillow, cheek on hand, facing the big-boned, ugly woman. She was apparently about eighteen years old. She wore a gray suit. Her hair was blonde and short, her face firm-featured and remarkably symmetrical. She did not look at the two men coming into the room.

Dundy spoke to the big-boned woman, while Spade was lighting his cigarette: "We want to ask you a couple of questions, too, Mrs. Hooper. You're Bliss's housekeeper, aren't you?"

The woman said, "I am." Her slightly harsh voice, the level gaze of her deep-set gray eyes, the stillness and size of her hands lying in her lap, all contributed to the impression she gave of resting strength.

"What do you know about this?"

"I don't know anything about it. I was let off this morning to go over to Oakland to my nephew's funeral, and when I got back you and the other gentlemen were here

36

and—and this had happened."

Dundy nodded, asked, "What do you think about it?"

"I don't know what to think," she replied simply.

"Didn't you know he expected it to happen?"

Now the girl suddenly stopped watching Mrs. Hooper. She sat up in bed, turning wide, excited eyes on Dundy, and asked, "What do you mean?"

"I mean what I said. He'd been threatened. He called up Mr. Spade"—he indicated Spade with a nod—"and told him so just a few minutes before he was killed."

"But who—?" she began.

"That's what we're asking you," Dundy said. "Who had that much against him?"

She stared at him in astonishment. "Nobody would—"

This time Spade interrupted her, speaking with a softness that made his words seem less brutal than they were. "Somebody did." When she turned her stare on him he asked, "You don't know of any threats?"

She shook her head from side to side with emphasis.

He looked at Mrs. Hooper. "You?"

"No, sir," she said.

He returned his attention to the girl. "Do you know Daniel Talbot?"

"Why, yes," she said. "He was here for dinner last night."

"Who is he?"

"I don't know, except that he lives in San Diego, and he and Father had some sort of business together. I'd never met him before."

"What sort of terms were they on?"

She frowned a little, said slowly, "Friendly."

Dundy spoke: "What business was your father in?"

"He was a financier."

"You mean a promoter?"

"Yes, I suppose you could call it that."

"Where is Talbot staying, or has he gone back to San Diego?"

"I don't know."

"What does he look like?"

She frowned again, thoughtfully. "He's kind of large, with a red face and white hair and a white mustache."

"Old?"

"I guess he must be sixty; fifty-five at least."

Dundy looked at Spade, who put the stub of his cigarette in a tray on the dressing table and took up the questioning. "How long since you've seen your uncle?"

Her face flushed. "You mean Uncle Ted?"

He nodded.

"Not since," she began, and bit her lip. Then she said, "Of course, you know. Not since he first got out of prison."

"He came here?"

"Yes."

"To see your father?"

"Of course."

"What sort of terms were they on?"

She opened her eyes wide. "Neither of them is very demonstrative," she said, "but they are brothers, and Father was giving him money to set him up in business again."

"Then they were on good terms?"

"Yes," she replied in the tone of one answering an unnecessary question.

"Where does he live?"

"On Post Street," she said, and gave a number.

"And you haven't seen him since?"

"No. He was shy, you know, about having been in prison—" She finished the sentence with a gesture of one hand.

Spade addressed Mrs. Hooper: "You've seen him since?"

"No, sir."

He pursed his lips, asked slowly, "Either of you know he was here this afternoon?"

They said, "No," together.

"Where did—?"

Someone knocked on the door.

Dundy said, "Come in."

Tom opened the door far enough to stick his head in. "His brother's here," he said.

The girl leaning forward, called, "Oh, Uncle Ted!"

A big blond man in brown appeared behind Tom. He was sunburned to an extent that made his teeth seem whiter, his clear eyes bluer, than they were.

He asked, "What's the matter, Miriam?"

"Father's dead," she said, and began to cry.

Dundy nodded at Tom, who stepped out of Theodore Bliss's way and let him come into the room.

A woman came in behind him, slowly, hesitantly. She was a tall woman in her late twenties, blonde, not quite plump. Her features were generous, her face pleasant and intelligent. She wore a small brown hat and a mink coat.

Bliss put an arm around his niece, kissed her forehead, sat on the bed beside her. "There, there," he said awkwardly.

She saw the blonde woman, stared through her tears at her for a moment, then said, "Oh, how do you do, Miss Barrow."

The blonde woman said, "I'm awfully sorry to—"

Bliss cleared his throat, and said, "She's Mrs. Bliss now. We were married this afternoon."

Dundy looked angrily at Spade. Spade, making a cigarette, seemed about to laugh.

Miriam Bliss, after a moment's surprised silence, said, "Oh, I do wish you all the happiness in the world." She turned to her uncle while his wife was murmuring "Thank you" and said, "And you too, Uncle Ted."

He patted her shoulder and squeezed her to him. He was looking questioningly at Spade and Dundy.

"Your brother died this afternoon," Dundy said. "He was murdered."

Mrs. Bliss caught her breath. Bliss's arm tightened around his niece with a little jerk, but there was not yet any change in his face. "Murdered?" he repeated uncomprehendingly.

"Yes." Dundy put his hands in his coat pockets. "You were here this afternoon."

Theodore Bliss paled a little under his sunburn, but said, "I was," steadily enough.

"How long?"

"About an hour. I got here about half past two and—" He turned to his wife. "It was almost half past three when I phoned you, wasn't it?"

She said, "Yes."

"Well, I left right after that."

"Did you have a date with him?" Dundy asked.

"No. I phoned his office"—he nodded at his wife—"and was told he'd left for home, so I came on up. I wanted to see him before Elise and I left, of course, and I wanted him to come to the wedding, but he couldn't. He said he was expecting somebody. We sat here and talked longer than I had intended, so I had to phone Elise to meet me at the Municipal Building."

After a thoughtful pause, Dundy asked, "What time?"

"That we met there?" Bliss looked inquiringly at his wife, who said, "It was just quarter to four." She laughed a little. "I got there first and I kept looking at my watch."

Bliss said very deliberately, "It was a few minutes after four that we were married. We had to wait for Judge Whitefield—about ten minutes, and it was a few more before we got started—to get through with the case he was hearing. You can check it up—Superior Court, Part Two, I think."

Spade whirled around and pointed at Tom. "Maybe you'd better check it up."

Tom said, "Oke," and went away from the door.

"If that's so, you're all right, Mr. Bliss," Dundy said, "but I have to ask you these things. Now, did your brother say who he was expecting?"

"No."

"Did he say anything about having been threatened?"

"No. He never talked much about his affairs to anybody, not even to me. Had he been threatened?"

Dundy's lips tightened a little. "Were you and he on intimate terms?"

"Friendly, if that's what you mean."

"Are you sure?" Dundy asked. "Are you sure neither of you held any grudge against the other?"

Theodore Bliss took his arm free from around his niece. Increasing pallor made his sunburned face yellowish. He said, "Everybody here knows about my having been in San Quentin. You can speak out, if that's what you're getting at."

"It is," Dundy said, and then, after a pause, "Well?"

Bliss stood up. "Well, what?" he asked impatiently. "Did I hold a grudge against him for that? No. Why should I? We were both in it. He could get out; I couldn't. I was sure of being convicted whether he was or not. Having him sent over with me wasn't going to make it any better for me. We talked it over and decided I'd go it alone, leaving him outside to pull things together. And he did. If you look up his bank

40

account you'll see he gave me a check for twenty-five thousand dollars two days after I was discharged from San Quentin and the registrar of the National Steel Corporation can tell you a thousand shares of stock have been transferred from his name to mine since then."

He smiled apologetically and sat down on the bed again. "I'm sorry. I know you have to ask things."

Dundy ignored the apology. "Do you know Daniel Talbot?" he asked.

Bliss said, "No."

His wife said, "I do; that is, I've seen him. He was in the office yesterday."

Dundy looked her up and down carefully before asking, "What office?"

"I am—I was Mr. Bliss's secretary, and—"

"Max Bliss's?"

"Yes, and a Daniel Talbot came in to see him yesterday afternoon, if it's the same one."

"What happened?"

She looked at her husband, who said, "If you know anything, for heaven's sake tell them."

She said, "But nothing really happened. I thought they were angry with each other at first, but when they left together they were laughing and talking, and before they went Mr. Bliss rang for me and told me to have Trapper—he's the bookkeeper— make out a check to Mr. Talbot's order."

"Did he?"

"Oh, yes. I took it in to him. It was for seventy-five hundred and some dollars."

"What was it for?"

She shook her head. "I don't know."

"If you were Bliss's secretary," Dundy insisted, "you must have some idea of what his business with Talbot was."

"But I haven't," she said. "I'd never even heard of him before."

Dundy looked at Spade. Spade's face was wooden. Dundy glowered at him, then put a question to the man on the bed: "What kind of necktie was your brother wearing when you saw him last?"

Bliss blinked, then stared distantly past Dundy, and finally shut his eyes. When he opened them he said, "It was green with—I'd know it if I saw it. Why?"

Mrs. Bliss said, "Narrow diagonal stripes of different shades of green. That's the one he had on at the office this morning."

"Where does he keep his neckties?" Dundy asked the housekeeper.

She rose, saying, "In a closet in his bedroom. I'll show you."

Dundy and the newly married Blisses followed her out.

Spade put his hat on the dressing table and asked Miriam Bliss, "What time did you go out?" He sat on the foot of her bed.

"Today? About one o'clock. I had a luncheon engagement for one and I was a little late, and then I went shopping, and then—" She broke off with a shudder.

"And then you came home at what time?" His voice was friendly, matter-of-fact.

"Some time after four, I guess."

"And what happened?"

"I f-found Father lying there and I phoned—I don't know whether I phoned downstairs or the police, and then I don't know what I did. I fainted or had hysterics or something, and the first thing I remember is coming to and finding those men here and Mrs. Hooper." She looked him full in the face now.

"You didn't phone a doctor?"

She lowered her eyes again. "No, I don't think so."

"Of course you wouldn't, if you knew he was dead," he said casually.

She was silent.

"You knew he was dead?" he asked.

She raised her eyes and looked blankly at him. "But he was dead," she said.

He smiled. "Of course; but what I'm getting at is, did you make sure before you phoned?"

She put a hand to her throat. "I don't remember what I did," she said earnestly. "I think I just knew he was dead."

He nodded understandingly. "And if you phoned the police it was because you knew he had been murdered."

She worked her hands together and looked at them and said, "I suppose so. It was awful. I don't know what I thought or did."

Spade leaned forward and made his voice low and persuasive. "I'm not a police detective, Miss Bliss. I was engaged by your father—a few minutes too late to save him. I am, in a way, working for you now, so if there is anything I can do—maybe something the police wouldn't—" He broke off as Dundy, followed by the Blisses and the housekeeper, returned to the room. "What luck?"

42

Dundy said, "The green tie's not there." His suspicious gaze darted from Spade to the girl. "Mrs. Hooper says the blue tie we found is one of half a dozen he just got from England."

Bliss asked, "What's the importance of the tie?"

Dundy scowled at him. "He was partly undressed when we found him. The tie with his clothes had never been worn."

"Couldn't he have been changing clothes when whoever killed him came, and was killed before he had finished dressing?"

Dundy's scowl deepened. "Yes, but what did he do with the green tie? Eat it?"

Spade said, "He wasn't changing clothes. If you'll look at the shirt collar you'll see he must've had it on when he was choked."

Tom came to the door. "Checks all right," he told Dundy. "The judge and a bailiff named Kittredge say they were there from about a quarter to four till five or ten minutes after. I told Kittredge to come over and take a look at them to make sure they're the same ones."

Dundy said, "Right," without turning his head and took the penciled threat signed with the T in a star from his pocket. He folded it so only the signature was visible. Then he asked, "Anybody know what this is?"

Miriam Bliss left the bed to join the others in looking at it. From it they looked at one another blankly.

"Anybody know anything about it?" Dundy asked.

Mrs. Hooper said, "It's like what was on poor Mr. Bliss's chest, but—" The others said, "No."

"Anybody ever seen anything like it before?"

They said they had not.

Dundy said, "All right. Wait here. Maybe I'll have something else to ask you after a while."

Spade said, "Just a minute. Mr. Bliss, how long have you known Mrs. Bliss?"

Bliss looked curiously at Spade. "Since I got out of prison," he replied somewhat cautiously. "Why?"

"Just since last month," Spade said as if to himself. "Meet her through your brother?"

"Of course—in his office. Why?"

"And at the Municipal Building this afternoon, were you together all the time?"

"Yes, certainly." Bliss spoke sharply. "What are you getting at?"

Spade smiled at him, a friendly smile. "I have to ask things," he said.

Bliss smiled too. "It's all right." His smile broadened. "As a matter of fact, I'm a liar. We weren't actually together all the time. I went out into the corridor to smoke a cigarette, but I assure you every time I looked through the glass of the door I could see her still sitting in the courtroom where I had left her."

Spade's smile was as light as Bliss's. Nevertheless, he asked, "And when you weren't looking through the glass you were in sight of the door? She couldn't've left the courtroom without your seeing her?"

Bliss's smile went away. "Of course she couldn't," he said, "and I wasn't out there more than five minutes."

Spade said, "Thanks," and followed Dundy into the living-room, shutting the door behind him.

Dundy looked sidewise at Spade. "Anything to it?"

Spade shrugged.

Max Bliss's body had been removed. Besides the man at the secrétaire and the gray-faced man, two Filipino boys in plum-colored uniforms were in the room. They sat close together on the sofa.

Dundy said, "Mack, I want to find a green necktie. I want this house taken apart, this block taken apart, and the whole neighborhood taken apart till you find it. Get what men you need."

The man at the secrétaire rose, said "Right," pulled his hat down over his eyes, and went out.

Dundy scowled at the Filipinos. "Which of you saw the man in brown?"

The smaller stood up. "Me, sir."

Dundy opened the bedroom door and said, "Bliss."

Bliss came to the door.

The Filipino's face lighted up. "Yes, sir, him."

Dundy shut the door in Bliss's face. "Sit down."

The boy sat down hastily.

Dundy stared gloomily at the boys until they began to fidget. Then, "Who else did you bring up to this apartment this afternoon?"

They shook their heads in unison from side to side. "Nobody else, sir," the smaller one said. A desperately ingratiating smile stretched his mouth wide across his face.

Dundy took a threatening step towards them. "Nuts!" he snarled. "You brought up Miss Bliss."

The larger boy's head bobbed up and down. "Yes, sir. Yes, sir. I bring them up. I think you mean other people." He too tried a smile.

Dundy was glaring at him. "Never mind what you think I mean. Tell me what I ask. Now, what do you mean by 'them'?"

The boy's smile died under the glare. He looked at the floor between his feet and said, "Miss Bliss and the gentleman."

"What gentleman? The gentleman in there?" He jerked his head toward the door he had shut on Bliss.

"No, sir. Another gentleman, not an American gentleman." He had raised his head again and now brightness came back into his face. "I think he is Armenian."

"Why?"

"Because he not like us Americans, not talk like us."

Spade laughed, asked, "Ever seen an Armenian?"

"No, sir. That is why I think—" He shut his mouth with a click as Dundy made a growling noise in his throat.

"What'd he look like?" Dundy asked.

The boy lifted his shoulders, spread his hands. "He tall, like this gentleman." He indicated Spade. "Got dark hair, dark mustache. Very"—he frowned earnestly—"very nice clothes. Very nice-looking man. Cane, gloves, spats, even, and—"

"Young?" Dundy asked.

The head went up and down again. "Young, yes, sir."

"When did he leave?"

"Five minutes," the boy replied.

Dundy made a chewing motion with his jaws, then asked, "What time did they come in?"

The boy spread his hands, lifted his shoulders again. "Four o'clock—maybe ten minutes after."

"Did you bring anybody else up before we got here?"

The Filipinos shook their heads in unison once more.

Dundy spoke out the side of his mouth to Spade: "Get her."

Spade opened the bedroom door, bowed slightly, said, "Will you come out a moment, Miss Bliss?"

"What is it?" she asked wearily.

"Just for a moment," he said, holding the door open. Then he suddenly added, "And you'd better come along, too, Mr. Bliss."

Miriam Bliss came slowly into the living-room followed by her uncle, and Spade shut the door behind them. Miss Bliss's lower lip twitched a little when she saw the elevator boys. She looked apprehensively at Dundy.

He asked, "What's this fiddlededee about the man that came in with you?"

Her lower lip twitched again. "Wh-what?" She tried to put bewilderment on her face. Theodore Bliss hastily crossed the room, stood for a moment before her as if he intended to say something, and then, apparently changing his mind, took up a position behind her, his arms crossed over the back of a chair.

"The man who came in with you," Dundy said harshly, rapidly. "Who is he? Where is he? Why'd he leave? Why didn't you say anything about him?"

The girl put her hands over her face and began to cry. "He didn't have anything to do with it," she blubbered through her hands. "He didn't, and it would just make trouble for him."

"Nice boy," Dundy said. "So, to keep his name out of the newspapers, he runs off and leaves you alone with your murdered father."

She took her hands away from her face. "Oh, but he had to," she cried. "His wife is so jealous, and if she knew he had been with me again she'd certainly divorce him, and he hasn't a cent in the world of his own."

Dundy looked at Spade. Spade looked at the goggling Filipinos and jerked a thumb at the outer door. "Scram," he said. They went out quickly.

"And who is this gem?" Dundy asked the girl.

"But he didn't have any—"

"Who is he?"

Her shoulders drooped a little and she lowered her eyes. "His name is Boris Smekalov," she said wearily.

"Spell it."

She spelled it.

"Where does he live?"

"At the St. Mark Hotel."

"Does he do anything for a living except marry money?"

Anger came into her face as she raised it, but went away as quickly. "He doesn't do anything," she said.

Dundy wheeled to address the gray-faced man. "Get him."

46

The gray-faced man grunted and went out.

Dundy faced the girl again. "You and this Smekalov in love with each other?"

Her face became scornful. She looked at him with scornful eyes and said nothing.

He said, "Now your father's dead, will you have enough money for him to marry if his wife divorces him?"

She covered her face with her hands.

He said, "Now your father's dead, will—?"

Spade, leaning far over, caught her as she fell. He lifted her easily and carried her into the bedroom. When he came back he shut the door behind him and leaned against it. "Whatever the rest of it was," he said, "the faint's a phony."

"Everything's a phony," Dundy growled.

Spade grinned mockingly. "There ought to be a law making criminals give themselves up."

Mr. Bliss smiled and sat down at his brother's desk by the window.

Dundy's voice was disagreeable. "You got nothing to worry about," he said to Spade. "Even your client's dead and can't complain. But if I don't come across I've got to stand for riding from the captain, the chief, the newspapers, and heaven knows who all."

"Stay with it," Spade said soothingly; "you'll catch a murderer sooner or later yet." His face became serious except for the lights in his yellow-gray eyes. "I don't want to run this job up any more alleys than we have to, but don't you think we ought to check up on the funeral the housekeeper said she went to? There's something funny about that woman."

After looking suspiciously at Spade for a moment, Dundy nodded, and said, "Tom'll do it."

Spade turned about and, shaking his finger at Tom, said, "It's a ten-to-one bet there wasn't any funeral. Check on it ... don't miss a trick."

Then he opened the bedroom door and called Mrs. Hooper. "Sergeant Polhaus wants some information from you," he told her.

While Tom was writing down names and addresses that the woman gave him, Spade sat on the sofa and made and smoked a cigarette, and Dundy walked the floor slowly, scowling at the rug. With Spade's approval, Theodore Bliss rose and rejoined his wife in the bedroom.

Presently Tom put his note book in his pocket, said, "Thank you," to the housekeeper, "Be seeing you," to Spade and Dundy, and left the apartment.

The housekeeper stood where he had left her, ugly, strong, serene, patient.

Spade twisted himself around on the sofa until he was looking into her deep-set, steady eyes. "Don't worry about that," he said, flirting a hand toward the door Tom had gone through. "Just routine." He pursed his lips, asked, "What do you honestly think of this thing, Mrs. Hooper?"

She replied calmly, in her strong, somewhat harsh voice, "I think it's the judgment of God."

Dundy stopped pacing the floor.

Spade said, "What?"

There was certainty and no excitement in her voice: "The wages of sin is death."

Dundy began to advance towards Mrs. Hooper in the manner of one stalking game. Spade waved him back with a hand which the sofa hid from the woman. His face and voice showed interest, but were now as composed as the woman's. "Sin?" he asked.

She said, "'Whosoever shall offend one of these little ones that believe in me, it were better for him that a millstone were hanged around his neck, and he were cast into the sea.'" She spoke, not as if quoting, but as if saying something she believed.

Dundy barked a question at her: "What little one?"

She turned her grave gray eyes on him, then looked past him at the bedroom door.

"Her," she said; "Miriam."

Dundy frowned at her. "His daughter?"

The woman said, "Yes, his own adopted daughter."

Angry blood mottled Dundy's square face. "What the heck is this?" he demanded. He shook his head as if to free it from some clinging thing. "She's not really his daughter?"

The woman's serenity was in no way disturbed by his anger. "No. His wife was an invalid most of her life. They didn't have any children."

Dundy moved his jaws as if chewing for a moment and when he spoke again his voice was cooler. "What did he do to her?"

"I don't know," she said, "but I truly believe that when the truth's found out you'll see that the money her father—I mean her real father—left her has been—"

Spade interrupted her, taking pains to speak very clearly, moving one hand in small circles with his words. "You mean you don't actually know he's been gypping her? You just suspect it?"

She put a hand over her heart. "I know it here," she replied calmly.

Dundy looked at Spade, Spade at Dundy, and Spade's eyes were shiny with not altogether pleasant merriment. Dundy cleared his throat and addressed the woman

48

again. "And you think this"—he waved a hand at the floor where the dead man had lain—"was the judgment of God, huh?"

"I do."

He kept all but the barest trace of craftiness out of his eyes. "Then whoever did it was just acting as the hand of God?"

"It's not for me to say," she replied.

Red began to mottle his face again.

"That'll be all right now," he said in a choking voice, but by the time she had reached the bedroom door his eyes became alert again and he called, "Wait a minute." And when they were facing each other: "Listen, do you happen to be a Rosicrucian?"

"I wish to be nothing but a Christian."

He growled, "All right, all right," and turned his back on her. She went into the bedroom and shut the door. He wiped his forehead with the palm of his right hand and complained wearily, "Great Scott, what a family."

Spade shrugged. "Try investigating your own some time."

Dundy's face whitened. His lips, almost colorless, came back tight over his teeth. He balled his fists and lunged towards Spade. "What do you—?" The pleasantly surprised look on Spade's face stopped him. He averted his eyes, wet his lips with the tip of his tongue, looked at Spade again and away, essayed an embarrassed smile, and mumbled, "You mean any family. Uh-huh, I guess so." He turned hastily towards the corridor door as the doorbell rang.

The amusement twitching Spade's face accentuated his likeness to a blond satan.

An amiable, drawling voice came in through the corridor door: "I'm Jim Kittredge, Superior Court. I was told to come over here."

Dundy's voice: "Yes, come in."

Kittredge was a roly-poly ruddy man in too-tight clothes with the shine of age on them. He nodded at Spade and said, "I remember you, Mr. Spade, from the Burke-Harris suit."

Spade said, "Sure," and stood up to shake hands with him.

Dundy had gone to the bedroom door to call Theodore Bliss and his wife. Kittredge looked at them, smiled at them amiably, said, "How do you do?" and turned to Dundy. "That's them, all right." He looked around as if for a place to spit, found none, and said, "It was just about ten minutes to four that the gentleman there came in the courtroom and asked me how long His Honor would be, and I told him about ten minutes, and they waited there; and right after court adjourned at four o'clock we married them."

Dundy said, "Thanks." He sent Kittredge away, the Blisses back to the bedroom, scowled with dissatisfaction at Spade, and said, "So what?"

Spade, sitting down again, replied, "So you couldn't get from here to the Municipal Building in less than fifteen minutes on a bet, so he couldn't've ducked back here while he was waiting for the judge, and he couldn't have hustled over here to do it after the wedding and before Miriam arrived."

The dissatisfaction in Dundy's face increased. He opened his mouth, but shut it in silence when the gray-faced man came in with a tall, slender, pale young man who fitted the description the Filipino had given of Miriam Bliss's companion.

The gray-faced man said, "Lieutenant Dundy, Mr. Spade, Mr. Boris—uh—Smekalov."

Dundy nodded curtly.

Smekalov began to speak immediately. His accent was not heavy enough to trouble his hearers much, though his r's sounded more like w's. "Lieutenant, I must beg of you that you keep this confidential. If it should get out it will ruin me, Lieutenant, ruin me completely and most unjustly. I am most innocent, sir, I assure you, in heart, spirit, and deed, not only innocent, but in no way whatever connected with any part of the whole horrible matter. There is no—"

"Wait a minute." Dundy prodded Smekalov's chest with a blunt finger. "Nobody's said anything about you being mixed up in anything—but it'd looked better if you'd stuck around."

The young man spread his arms, his palms forward, in an expansive gesture. "But what can I do? I have a wife who—" He shook his head, violently. "It is impossible. I cannot do it."

The gray-faced man said to Spade in an inadequately subdued voice, "Goofy, these Russians."

Dundy screwed up his eyes at Smekalov and made his voice judicial. "You've probably," he said, "put yourself in a pretty tough spot."

Smekalov seemed about to cry. "But only put yourself in my place," he begged, "and you—"

"Wouldn't want to." Dundy seemed, in his callous way, sorry for the young man. "Murder's nothing to play with in this country."

"Murder! But I tell you, Lieutenant, I happen' to enter into this situation by the merest mischance only. I am not—"

"You mean you came in here with Miss Bliss by accident?"

The young man looked as if he would like to say "Yes." He said, "No," slowly, then went on with increasing rapidity: "But that was nothing, sir, nothing at all. We had

50

been to lunch. I escorted her home and she said, 'Will you come in for a cocktail?' and I would. That is all, I give you my word." He held out his hands, palms up. "Could it not have happened so to you?" He moved his hands in Spade's direction. "To you?"

Spade said, "A lot of things happen to me. Did Bliss know you were running around with his daughter?"

"He knew we were friends, yes."

"Did he know you had a wife?"

Smekalov said cautiously, "I do not think so."

Dundy said, "You know he didn't."

Smekalov moistened his lips and did not contradict the lieutenant.

Dundy asked, "What do you think he'd've done if he found out?"

"I do not know, sir."

Dundy stepped close to the young man and spoke through his teeth in a harsh, deliberate voice: "What *did* he do when he found out?"

The young man retreated a step, his face white and frightened.

The bedroom door opened and Miriam Bliss came into the room. "Why don't you leave him alone?" she asked indignantly. "I told you he had nothing to do with it. I told you he didn't know anything about it." She was beside Smekalov now and had one of his hands in hers. "You're simply making trouble for him without doing a bit of good. I'm awfully sorry, Boris, I tried to keep them from bothering you."

The young man mumbled unintelligibly.

"You tried, all right," Dundy agreed. He addressed Spade: "Could it've been like this, Sam? Bliss found out about the wife, knew they had the lunch date, came home early to meet them when they came in, threatened to tell the wife, and was choked to stop him." He looked sidewise at the girl. "Now, if you want to fake another faint, hop to it."

The young man screamed and flung himself at Dundy, clawing with both hands. Dundy grunted—"Uh!"—and struck him in the face with a heavy fist. The young man went backwards across the room until he collided with a chair. He and the chair went down on the floor together. Dundy said to the gray-faced man, "Take him down to the Hall—material witness."

The gray-faced man said, "Oke," picked up Smekalov's hat, and went over to help pick him up.

Theodore Bliss, his wife, and the housekeeper had come to the door Miriam Bliss had left open. Miriam Bliss was crying, stamping her foot, threatening Dundy: "I'll

51

report you, you coward. You had no right to ..." and so on. Nobody paid much attention to her; they watched the gray-faced man help Smekalov to his feet, take him away. Smekalov's nose and mouth were red smears.

Then Dundy said, "Hush," negligently to Miriam Bliss and took a slip of paper from his pocket. "I got a list of the calls from here today. Sing out when you recognize them."

He read a telephone number.

Mrs. Hooper said, "That is the butcher. I phoned him before I left this morning." She said the next number Dundy read was the grocer's.

He read another.

"That's the St. Mark," Miriam Bliss said. "I called up Boris." She identified two more numbers as those of friends she had called.

The sixth number, Bliss said, was his brother's office. "Probably my call to Elise to ask her to meet me."

Spade said "Mine," to the seventh number, and Dundy said, "That last one's police emergency." He put the slip back in his pocket.

Spade said cheerfully, "And that gets us a lot of places."

The doorbell rang.

Dundy went to the door. He and another man could be heard talking in voices too low for their words to be recognized in the living room.

The telephone rang. Spade answered it. "Hello.... No, this is Spade. Wait a min—All right." He listened. "Right, I'll tell him.... I don't know. I'll have him call you.... Right."

When he turned from the telephone Dundy was standing, hands behind him, in the vestibule doorway. Spade said, "O'Gar says your Russian went completely nuts on the way to the Hall. They had to shove him into a strait-jacket."

"He ought to been there long ago," Dundy growled. "Come here."

Spade followed Dundy into the vestibule. A uniformed policeman stood in the outer doorway.

Dundy brought his hands from behind him. In one was a necktie with narrow diagonal stripes in varying shades of green, in the other was a platinum scarfpin in the shape of a crescent set with small diamonds.

Spade bent over to look at three small, irregular spots on the tie. "Blood?"

"Or dirt," Dundy said. "He found them crumpled up in a newspaper in the rubbish can on the corner."

"Yes, sir," the uniformed man said proudly; "there I found them, all wadded up in—" He stopped because nobody was paying any attention to him.

"Blood's better," Spade was saying. "It gives a reason for taking the tie away. Let's go in and talk to people."

Dundy stuffed the tie in one pocket, thrust his hand holding the pin into another. "Right—and we'll call it blood."

They went into the living-room. Dundy looked from Bliss to Bliss's wife, to Bliss's niece, to the housekeeper, as if he did not like any of them. He took his fist from his pocket, thrust it straight out in front of him, and opened it to show the crescent pin lying in his hand. "What's that?" he demanded.

Miriam Bliss was the first to speak. "Why, it's Father's pin," she said.

"So it is?" he said disagreeably. "And did he have it on today?"

"He always wore it." She turned to the others for confirmation.

Mrs. Bliss said, "Yes," while the others nodded.

"Where did you find it?" the girl asked.

Dundy was surveying them one by one again, as if he liked them less than ever. His face was red. "He always wore it," he said angrily, "but there wasn't one of you could say, 'Father always wore a pin. Where is it?' No, we got to wait till it turns up before we can get a word out of you about it."

Bliss said, "Be fair. How were we to know—?"

"Never mind what you were to know," Dundy said. "It's coming around to the point where I'm going to do some talking about what I know." He took the green necktie from his pocket. "This is his tie?"

Mrs. Hooper said, "Yes, sir."

Dundy said, "Well, it's got blood on it, and it's not his blood, because he didn't have a scratch on him that we could see." He looked narrow-eyed from one to another of them. "Now, suppose you were trying to choke a man that wore a scarfpin and he was wrestling with you, and—"

He broke off to look at Spade.

Spade had crossed to where Mrs. Hooper was standing. Her big hands were clasped in front of her. He took her right hand, turned it over, took the wadded handkerchief from her palm, and there was a two-inch-long fresh scratch in the flesh.

She had passively allowed him to examine her hand. Her mien lost none of its tranquillity now. She said nothing.

"Well?" he asked.

"I scratched it on Miss Miriam's pin fixing her on the bed when she fainted," the housekeeper said calmly.

Dundy's laugh was brief, bitter. "It'll hang you just the same," he said.

There was no change in the woman's face. "The Lord's will be done," she replied.

Spade made a peculiar noise in his throat as he dropped her hand. "Well, let's see how we stand." He grinned at Dundy. "You don't like that star-T, do you?"

Dundy said, "Not by a long shot."

"Neither do I," Spade said. "The Talbot threat was probably on the level, but that debt seems to have been squared. Now—Wait a minute." He went to the telephone and called his office. "The tie thing looked pretty funny, too, for a while," he said while he waited, "but I guess the blood takes care of that."

He spoke into the telephone: "Hello, Effie. Listen: Within half an hour or so of the time Bliss called me, did you get any call that maybe wasn't on the level? Anything that could have been a stall ... Yes, before ... Think now."

He put his hand over the mouthpiece and said to Dundy, "There's a lot of deviltry going on in this world."

He spoke into the telephone again: "Yes?... Yes ... Kruger?... Yes. Man or woman?... Thanks.... No, I'll be through in half an hour. Wait for me and I'll buy your dinner. 'By."

He turned away from the telephone. "About half an hour before Bliss phoned, a man called my office and asked for Mr. Kruger."

Dundy frowned. "So what?"

"Kruger wasn't there."

Dundy's frown deepened. "Who's Kruger?"

"I don't know," Spade said blandly. "I never heard of him." He took tobacco and cigarette papers from his pockets. "All right, Bliss, where's your scratch?"

Theodore Bliss said, "What?" while the others stared blankly at Spade.

"Your scratch," Spade repeated in a consciously patient tone. His attention was on the cigarette he was making. "The place where your brother's pin gouged you when you were choking him."

"Are you crazy?" Bliss demanded. "I was—"

"Uh-huh, you were being married when he was killed. You were not." Spade moistened the edge of his cigarette paper and smoothed it with his forefingers.

Mrs. Bliss spoke now, stammering a little: "But he—but Max Bliss called—"

"Who says Max Bliss called me?" Spade asked. "I don't know that. I wouldn't know his voice. All I know is a man called me and said he was Max Bliss. Anybody could say that."

"But the telephone records here show the call came from here," she protested.

He shook his head and smiled. "They show I had a call from here, and I did, but not that one. I told you somebody called up half an hour or so before the supposed Max Bliss call and asked for Mr. Kruger." He nodded at Theodore Bliss. "He was smart enough to get a call from this apartment to my office on the record before he left to meet you."

She stared from Spade to her husband with dumfounded blue eyes.

Her husband said lightly, "It's nonsense, my dear. You know—"

Spade did not let him finish that sentence. "You know he went out to smoke a cigarette in the corridor while waiting for the judge, and he knew there were telephone booths in the corridor. A minute would be all he needed." He lit his cigarette and returned his lighter to his pocket.

Bliss said, "Nonsense!" more sharply. "Why should I want to kill Max?" He smiled reassuringly into his wife's horrified eyes. "Don't let this disturb you, dear. Police methods are sometimes—"

"All right," Spade said, "let's look you over for scratches."

Bliss wheeled to face him more directly. "Damned if you will!" He put a hand behind him.

Spade, wooden-faced and dreamy-eyed, came forward.

Spade and Effie Perine sat at a small table in Julius's Castle on Telegraph Hill. Through the window beside them ferryboats could be seen carrying lights to and from the cities' lights on the other side of the bay.

"... hadn't gone there to kill him, chances are," Spade was saying; "just to shake him down for some more money; but when the fight started, once he got his hands on his throat, I guess, his grudge was too hot in him for him to let go till Max was dead. Understand, I'm just putting together what the evidence says, and what we got out of his wife, and the not much that we got out of him."

Effie nodded. "She's a nice, loyal wife."

Spade drank coffee, shrugged. "What for? She knows now that he made his play for her only because she was Max's secretary. She knows that when he took out the marriage license a couple of weeks ago it was only to string her along so she'd get him the photostatic copies of the records that tied Max up with the Graystone Loan swindle. She knows—Well, she knows she wasn't just helping an injured innocent to clear his good name."

He took another sip of coffee. "So he calls on his brother this afternoon to hold San Quentin over his head for a price again, and there's a fight, and he kills him, and gets his wrist scratched by the pin while he's choking him. Blood on the tie, a scratch on his wrist—that won't do. He takes the tie off the corpse and hunts up another, because the absence of a tie will set the police to thinking. He gets a bad break there: Max's new ties are on the front of the rack, and he grabs the first one he comes to. All right. Now he's got to put it around the dead man's neck—or wait—he gets a better idea. Pull off some more clothes and puzzle the police. The tie'll be just as inconspicuous off as on, if the shirt's off too. Undressing him, he gets another idea. He'll give the police something else to worry about, so he draws a mystic sign he has seen somewhere on the dead man's chest."

Spade emptied his cup, set it down, and went on: "By now he's getting to be a regular master-mind at bewildering the police. A threatening letter signed with the thing on Max's chest. The afternoon mail is on the desk. One envelope's as good as another so long as it's typewritten and has no return address, but the one from France adds a touch of the foreign, so out comes the original letter and in goes the threat. He's overdoing it now; see? He's giving us so much that's wrong that we can't help suspecting things that seem all right—the phone call, for instance.

"Well, he's ready for the phone calls now—his alibi. He picks my name out of the private detectives in the phone book and does the Mr. Kruger trick; but that's after he calls the blonde Elise and tells her that not only have the obstacles to their marriage been removed, but he's had an offer to go in business in New York and has to leave right away, and will she meet him in fifteen minutes and get married? There's more than just an alibi to that. He wants to make sure *she* is dead sure he didn't kill Max, because she knows he doesn't like Max, and he doesn't want her to think he was just stringing her along to get the dope on Max, because she might be able to put two and two together and get something like the right answer.

"With that taken care of, he's ready to leave. He goes out quite openly, with only one thing to worry about now—the tie and pin in his pocket. He takes the pin along because he's not sure the police mightn't find traces of blood around the setting of the stones, no matter how carefully he wipes it. On his way out he picks up a newspaper —buys one from the newsboy he meets at the street door—wads tie and pin up in a piece of it, and drops it in the rubbish can at the corner. That seems all right. No reason for the police to look for the tie. No reason for the street cleaner who empties the can to investigate a crumpled piece of newspaper, and if something does go wrong—what the deuce!—the murderer dropped it there, but he, Theodore, can't be the murderer, because he's going to have an alibi.

"Then he jumps in his car and drives to the Municipal Building. He knows there are plenty of phones there and he can always say he's got to wash his hands, but it turns out he doesn't have to. While they're waiting for the judge to get through with a case he goes out to smoke a cigarette, and there you are—'Mr. Spade, this is Max Bliss and I've been threatened.'"

Effie Perine nodded, then asked, "Why do you suppose he picked on a private detective instead of the police?"

"Playing safe. If the body had been found, meanwhile, the police might've heard of it and trace the call. A private detective wouldn't be likely to hear about it till he read it in the papers."

She laughed, then said, "And that was your luck."

"Luck? I don't know." He looked gloomily at the back of his left hand. "I hurt a knuckle stopping him and the job only lasted an afternoon. Chances are whoever's handling the estate'll raise hob if I send them a bill for any decent amount of money." He raised a hand to attract the waiter's attention. "Oh, well, better luck next time. Want to catch a movie or have you got something else to do?"

THE ASSISTANT MURDERER

Gold on the door, edged with black, said ALEXANDER RUSH, PRIVATE DETECTIVE. Inside, an ugly man sat tilted back in a chair, his feet on a yellow desk.

The office was in no way lovely. Its furnishings were few and old with the shabby age of second-handom. A shredding square of dun carpet covered the floor. On one buff wall hung a framed certificate that licensed Alexander Rush to pursue the calling of private detective in the city of Baltimore in accordance with certain red-numbered regulations. A map of the city hung on another wall. Beneath the map a frail bookcase, small as it was, gaped emptily around its contents: a yellowish railway guide, a smaller hotel directory, and street and telephone directories for Baltimore, Washington and Philadelphia. An insecure oaken clothes-tree held up a black derby and a black overcoat beside a white sink in one corner. The four chairs in the room were unrelated to one another in everything except age. The desk's scarred top held, in addition to the proprietor's feet, a telephone, a black-clotted inkwell, a disarray of papers having generally to do with criminals who had escaped from one prison or another, and a grayed ashtray that held as much ash and as many black cigar stumps as a tray of its size could expect to hold.

An ugly office—the proprietor was uglier.

His head was squatly pear-shaped. Excessively heavy, wide, blunt at the jaw, it narrowed as it rose to the close-cropped, erect grizzled hair that sprouted above a low, slanting forehead. His complexion was of a rich darkish red, his skin tough in texture and rounded over thick cushions of fat. These fundamental inelegancies were by no means all his ugliness. Things had been done to his features.

One way you looked at his nose, you said it was crooked. Another way, you said it could not be crooked; it had no shape at all. Whatever your opinion of its form, you could not deny its color. Veins had been broken to pencil its already florid surface with brilliant red stars and curls and puzzling scrawls that looked as if they must have some secret meanings. His lips were thick, tough-skinned. Between them showed the brassy glint of two solid rows of gold teeth, the lower row lapping the upper, so undershot was the bulging jaw. His eyes—small, deep-set and pale blue of iris—were bloodshot to a degree that made you think he had a heavy cold. His ears accounted for some of his earlier years: they were the thickened, twisted cauliflower ears of the pugilist.

A man of forty-something, ugly, sitting tilted back in his chair, feet on desk.

The gilt-labeled door opened and another man came into the office. Perhaps ten years younger than the man at the desk, he was, roughly speaking, everything that one was not. Fairly tall, slender, fair-skinned, brown-eyed, he would have been as little likely to catch your eye in a gambling house as in an art gallery. His clothes—suit and hat were gray—were fresh and properly pressed, and even fashionable in that inconspicuous manner which is one sort of taste. His face was likewise unobtrusive, which was surprising when you considered how narrowly it missed handsomeness through the least meagerness of mouth—a mark of the too cautious man.

Two steps into the office he hesitated, brown eyes glancing from shabby furnishings to ill-visaged proprietor. So much ugliness seemed to disconcert the man in gray. An apologetic smile began on his lips, as if he were about to murmur, "I beg your pardon, I'm in the wrong office."

But when he finally spoke it was otherwise. He took another step forward, asking uncertainly:

"You are Mr. Rush?"

"Yeah." The detective's voice was hoarse with a choking harshness that seemed to corroborate the heavy-cold testimony of his eyes. He put his feet down on the floor and jerked a fat, red hand at a chair. "Sit down, sir."

The man in gray sat down, tentatively upright on the chair's front edge.

"Now what can I do for you?" Alec Rush croaked amiably.

"I want—I wish—I would like—" and further than that the man in gray said nothing.

"Maybe you'd better just tell me what's wrong," the detective suggested. "Then I'll know what you want of me," and he smiled.

There was kindliness in Alec Rush's smile, and it was not easily resisted. True, his smile was a horrible grimace out of a nightmare, but that was its charm. When your gentle-countenanced man smiles there is small gain: his smile expresses little more than his reposed face. But when Alec Rush distorted his ogre's mask so that jovial friendliness peeped incongruously from his savage red eyes, from his brutal metal-studded mouth—then that was a heartening, a winning thing.

58

"Yes, I daresay that would be better." The man in gray sat back in his chair, more comfortably, less transiently. "Yesterday on Fayette Street, I met a—a young woman I know. I hadn't—we hadn't met for several months. That isn't really pertinent, however. But after we separated—we had talked for a few minutes—I saw a man. That is, he came out of a doorway and went down the street in the same direction she had taken, and I got the idea he was following her. She turned into Liberty Street and he did likewise. Countless people walk along that same route, and the idea that he was following her seemed fantastic, so much so that I dismissed it and went on about my business.

"But I couldn't get the notion out of my head. It seemed to me there had been something peculiarly intent in his carriage, and no matter how much I told myself the notion was absurd, it persisted in worrying me. So last night, having nothing especial to do, I drove out to the neighborhood of—of the young woman's house. And I saw the same man again. He was standing on a corner two blocks from her house. It was the same man—I'm certain of it. I tried to watch him, but while I was finding a place for my car he disappeared and I did not see him again. Those are the circumstances. Now will you look into it, learn if he is actually following her, and why?"

"Sure," the detective agreed hoarsely, "but didn't you say anything to the lady or to any of her family?"

The man in gray fidgeted in his chair and looked at the stringy dun carpet.

"No, I didn't. I didn't want to disturb her, frighten her, and still don't. After all, it may be no more than a meaningless coincidence, and—and—well—I don't—That's impossible! What I had in mind was for you to find out what is wrong, if anything, and remedy it without my appearing in the matter at all."

"Maybe, but, mind you, I'm not saying I will. I'd want to know more first."

"More? You mean more——"

"More about you and her."

"But there is nothing about us!" the man in gray protested. "It is exactly as I have told you. I might add that the young woman is—is married, and that until yesterday I had not seen her since her marriage."

"Then your interest in her is—?" The detective let the husky interrogation hang incompleted in the air.

"Of friendship—past friendship."

"Yeah. Now who is this young woman?"

The man in gray fidgeted again.

"See here, Rush," he said, coloring, "I'm perfectly willing to tell you, and shall, of course, but I don't want to tell you unless you are going to handle this thing for me. I mean I don't want to be bringing her name into it if—if you aren't. Will you?"

Alec Rush scratched his grizzled head with a stubby forefinger.

"I don't know," he growled. "That's what I'm trying to find out. I can't take a hold of a job that might be anything. I've got to know that you're on the up-and-up."

Puzzlement disturbed the clarity of the younger man's brown eyes.

"But I didn't think you'd be——" He broke off and looked away from the ugly man.

"Of course you didn't." A chuckle rasped in the detective's burly throat, the chuckle of a man touched in a once sore spot that is no longer tender. He raised a big hand to arrest his prospective client in the act of rising from his chair. "What you did, on a guess, was to go to one of the big agencies and tell 'em your story. They wouldn't touch it unless you cleared up the fishy points. Then you ran across my name, remembered I was chucked out of the department a couple of years ago. 'There's my man,' you said to yourself, 'a baby who won't be so choicy!'"

The man in gray protested with head and gesture and voice that this was not so. But his eyes were sheepish.

Alec Rush laughed harshly again and said, "No matter. I ain't sensitive about it. I can talk about politics, and being made the goat, and all that, but the records show the Board of Police Commissioners gave me the air for a list of crimes that would stretch from here to Canton Hollow. All right, sir! I'll take your job. It sounds phony, but maybe it ain't. It'll cost you fifteen a day and expenses."

"I can see that it sounds peculiar," the younger man assured the detective, "but you'll find that it's quite all right. You'll want a retainer, of course."

"Yes, say fifty."

The man in gray took five new ten-dollar bills from a pigskin billfold and put them on the desk. With a thick pen Alec Rush began to make muddy ink-marks on a receipt blank.

"Your name?" he asked.

"I would rather not. I'm not to appear in it, you know. My name would not be of importance, would it?"

Alec Rush put down his pen and frowned at his client.

"Now! Now!" he grumbled good-naturedly. "How am I going to do business with a man like you?"

The man in gray was sorry, even apologetic, but he was stubborn in his reticence. He would not give his name. Alec Rush growled and complained, but pocketed the five ten-dollar bills.

"It's in your favor, maybe," the detective admitted as he surrendered, "though it ain't to your credit. But if you were off-color I guess you'd have sense enough to fake a name. Now this young woman—who is she?"

"Mrs. Hubert Landow."

"Well, well, we've got a name at last! And where does Mrs. Landow live?"

"On Charles-Street Avenue," the man in gray said, and gave a number.

"Her description?"

"She is twenty-two or -three years old, rather tall, slender in an athletic way, with auburn hair, blue eyes and very white skin."

"And her husband? You know him?"

"I have seen him. He is about my age—thirty—but larger than I, a tall, broad-shouldered man of the clean-cut blond type."

"And your mystery man? What does he look like?"

"He's quite young, not more than twenty-two at the most, and not very large—medium size, perhaps, or a little under. He's very dark, with high cheekbones and a large nose. High, straight shoulders, too, but not broad. He walks with small, almost mincing, steps."

"Clothes?"

"He was wearing a brown suit and a tan cap when I saw him on Fayette Street yesterday afternoon. I suppose he wore the same last night, but I'm not positive."

"I suppose you'll drop in here for my reports," the detective wound up, "since I won't know where to send them to you?"

"Yes." The man in gray stood up and held out his hand. "I'm very grateful to you for undertaking this, Mr. Rush."

Alec Rush said that was all right. They shook hands, and the man in gray went out.

The ugly man waited until his client had had time to turn off into the corridor that led to the elevators. Then the detective said, "Now, Mr. Man!" got up from his chair, took his hat from the clothes-tree in the corner, locked his office door behind him, and ran down the back stairs.

He ran with the deceptive heavy agility of a bear. There was something bear-like, too, in the looseness with which his blue suit hung on his stout body, and in the set of his heavy shoulders—sloping, limber-jointed shoulders whose droop concealed much of their bulk.

He gained the ground floor in time to see the gray back of his client issuing into the street. In his wake Alec Rush sauntered. Two blocks, a turn to the left, another block and a turn to the right. The man in gray went into the office of a trust company that occupied the ground floor of a large office building.

The rest was the mere turning of a hand. Half a dollar to a porter: the man in gray was Ralph Millar, assistant cashier.

61

Darkness was settling in Charles-Street Avenue when Alec Rush, in a modest black coupé, drove past the address Ralph Millar had given him. The house was large in the dusk, spaced from its fellows as from the paving by moderate expanses of fenced lawn.

Alec Rush drove on, turned to the left at the first crossing, again to the left at the next, and at the next. For half an hour he guided his car along a many-angled turning and returning route until, when finally he stopped beside the curb at some distance from, but within sight of, the Landow house, he had driven through every piece of thoroughfare in the vicinity of that house.

He had not seen Millar's dark, high-shouldered young man.

Lights burned brightly in Charles-Street Avenue, and the night traffic began to purr southward into the city. Alec Rush's heavy body slumped against the wheel of his coupé while he filled its interior with pungent fog from a black cigar, and held patient, bloodshot eyes on what he could see of the Landow residence.

Three-quarters of an hour passed, and there was motion in the house. A limousine left the garage in the rear for the front door. A man and a woman, faintly distinguishable at that distance, left the house for the limousine. The limousine moved out into the cityward current. The third car behind it was Alec Rush's modest coupé.

Except for a perilous moment at North Avenue, when the interfering cross-stream of traffic threatened to separate him from his quarry, Alec Rush followed the limousine without difficulty. In front of a Howard Street theatre it discharged its freight: a youngish man and a young woman, both tall, evening-clad, and assuringly in agreement with the descriptions the detective had got from his client.

The Landows went into the already dark theatre while Alec Rush was buying his ticket. In the light of the first intermission he discovered them again. Leaving his seat for the rear of the auditorium, he found an angle from which he could study them for the remaining five minutes of illumination.

Hubert Landow's head was rather small for his stature, and the blond hair with which it was covered threatened each moment to escape from its imposed smoothness into crisp curls. His face, healthily ruddy, was handsome in a muscular, very masculine way, not indicative of any great mental nimbleness. His wife had that beauty which needs no cataloguing. However, her hair was auburn, her eyes blue, her skin white, and she looked a year or two older than the maximum twenty-three Millar had allowed her.

While the intermission lasted Hubert Landow talked to his wife eagerly, and his bright eyes were the eyes of a lover. Alec Rush could not see Mrs. Landow's eyes. He saw her replying now and again to her husband's words. Her profile showed no answering eagerness. She did not show she was bored.

Midway the last act, Alec Rush left the theatre to maneuver his coupé into a handy position from which to cover the Landows' departure. But their limousine did not pick them up when they left the theatre. They turned down Howard Street afoot, going to a rather garish second-class restaurant, where an abbreviated orchestra succeeded by main strength in concealing its smallness from the ear.

His coupé conveniently parked, Alec Rush found a table from which he could watch his subjects without being himself noticeable. Husband still wooed wife with incessant, eager talking. Wife was listless, polite, unkindled. Neither more than touched the food before them. They danced once, the woman's face as little touched by immediate interest as when she listened to her husband's words. A beautiful face, but empty.

The minute hand of Alec Rush's nickel-plated watch had scarcely begun its last climb of the day from where VI is inferred to XII when the Landows left the restaurant. The limousine—against its side a young Norfolk-jacketed Negro smoking—was two doors away. It bore them back to their house. The detective having seen them into the house, having seen the limousine into the garage, drove his coupé again around and around through the neighboring thoroughfares. And saw nothing of Millar's dark young man.

Then Alec Rush went home and to bed.

At eight o'clock the next morning ugly man and modest coupé were stationary in Charles-Street Avenue again. Male Charles-Street Avenue went with the sun on its left toward its offices. As the morning aged and the shadows grew shorter and thicker, so, generally, did the individuals who composed this morning procession. Eight-o'clock was frequently young and slender and brisk, Eight-thirty less so, Nine still less, and rear-guard Ten-o'clock was preponderantly neither young nor slender, and more often sluggish than brisk.

Into this rear guard, though physically he belonged to no later period than eight-thirty, a blue roadster carried Hubert Landow. His broad shoulders were blue-coated, his blond hair gray-capped, and he was alone in the roadster. With a glance around to make sure Millar's dark young man was not in sight, Alec Rush turned his coupé in the blue car's wake.

They rode swiftly into the city, down into its financial center, where Hubert Landow deserted his roadster before a Redwood Street stockbroker's office. The morning had become noon before Landow was in the street again, turning his roadster northward.

When shadowed and shadower came to rest again they were in Mount Royal Avenue. Landow got out of his car and strode briskly into a large apartment building. A block distant, Alec Rush lighted a black cigar and sat still in his coupé. Half an hour passed. Alec Rush turned his head and sank his gold teeth deep into his cigar.

Scarcely twenty feet behind the coupé, in the doorway of a garage, a dark young man with high cheekbones, high, straight shoulders, loitered. His nose was large. His suit was brown, as were the eyes with which he seemed to pay no especial attention to anything through the thin blue drift of smoke from the tip of a drooping cigarette.

Alec Rush took his cigar from his mouth to examine it, took a knife from his pocket to trim the bitten end, restored cigar to mouth and knife to pocket, and thereafter was as indifferent to all Mount Royal Avenue as the dark youth behind him. The one drowsed in his doorway. The other dozed in his car. And the afternoon crawled past one o'clock, past one-thirty.

Hubert Landow came out of the apartment building, vanished swiftly in his blue roadster. His going stirred neither of the motionless men, scarcely their eyes. Not until another fifteen minutes had gone did either of them move.

Then the dark youth left his doorway. He moved without haste, up the street, with short, almost mincing, steps. The back of Alec Rush's black-derbied head was to the youth when he passed the coupé, which may have been chance, for none could have said that the ugly man had so much as glanced at the other since his first sight of him. The dark young man let his eyes rest on the detective's back without interest as he passed. He went on up the street toward the apartment building Landow had visited, up its steps and out of sight into it.

When the dark young man had disappeared, Alec Rush threw away his cigar, stretched, yawned, and awakened the coupé's engine. Four blocks and two turnings from Mount Royal Avenue, he got out of the automobile, leaving it locked and empty in front of a gray stone church. He walked back to Mount Royal Avenue, to halt on a corner two blocks above his earlier position.

He had another half-hour of waiting before the dark young man appeared. Alec Rush was buying a cigar in a glass-fronted cigar store when the other passed. The young man boarded a street car at North Avenue and found a seat. The detective boarded the same car at the next corner and stood on the rear platform. Warned by an indicative forward hitching of the young man's shoulders and head, Alec Rush was the first passenger off the car at Madison Avenue, and the first aboard a southbound car there. And again, he was off first at Franklin Street.

The dark youth went straight to a rooming-house in this street, while the detective came to rest beside the window of a corner drug store specializing in theatrical make-up. There he loafed until half-past three. When the dark young man came into the street again it was to walk—Alec Rush behind him—to Eutaw Street, board a car, and ride to Camden Station.

There, in the waiting-room, the dark young man met a young woman who frowned and asked:

"Where in the hell have you been at?"

Passing them, the detective heard the petulant greeting, but the young man's reply was pitched too low for him to catch, nor did he hear anything else the young woman said. They talked for perhaps ten minutes, standing together in a deserted end of the waiting-room, so that Alec Rush could not have approached them without making himself conspicuous.

The young woman seemed to be impatient, urgent. The young man seemed to explain, to reassure. Now and then he gestured with the ugly, deft hands of a skilled mechanic. His companion became more agreeable. She was short, square, as if carved economically from a cube. Consistently, her nose also was short and her chin square. She had, on the whole, now that her earlier displeasure was passing, a merry face, a pert, pugnacious, rich-blooded face that advertised inexhaustible vitality. That advertisement was in every feature, from the live ends of her cut brown hair to the earth-gripping pose of her feet on the cement flooring. Her clothes were dark, quiet, expensive, but none too gracefully worn, hanging just the least bit bunchily here and there on her sturdy body.

Nodding vigorously several times, the young man at length tapped his cap-visor with two careless fingers and went out into the street. Alec Rush let him depart unshadowed. But when, walking slowly out to the iron train-shed gates, along them to the baggage window, thence to the street door, the young woman passed out of the station, the ugly man was behind her. He was still behind her when she joined the four o'clock shopping crowd at Lexington Street.

The young woman shopped with the whole-hearted air of one with nothing else on her mind. In the second department store she visited, Alec Rush left her looking at a display of laces while he moved as swiftly and directly as intervening shoppers would permit toward a tall, thick-shouldered, gray-haired woman in black, who seemed to be waiting for someone near the foot of a flight of stairs.

"Hello, Alec!" she said when he touched her arm, and her humorous eyes actually looked with pleasure at his uncouth face. "What are you doing in my territory?"

"Got a booster for you," he mumbled. "The chunky girl in blue at the lace counter. Make her?"

The store detective looked and nodded.

"Yes. Thanks, Alec. You're sure she's boosting, of course?"

"Now, Minnie!" he complained, his rasping voice throttled down to a metallic growl. "Would I be giving you a bum rumble? She went south with a couple of silk pieces, and it's more than likely she's got herself some lace by now."

"Um-hmm," said Minnie. "Well, when she sticks her foot on the sidewalk, I'll be with her."

Alec Rush put his hand on the store detective's arm again.

"I want a line on her," he said. "What do you say we tail her around and see what she's up to before we knock her over?"

"If it doesn't take all day," the woman agreed. And when the chunky girl in blue presently left the lace counter and the store, the detectives followed, into another store, ranging too far behind her to see any thieving she might have done, content to keep her under surveillance. From this last store their prey went down to where Pratt

Street was dingiest, into a dingy three-story house of furnished flats.

Two blocks away a policeman was turning a corner.

"Take a plant on the joint while I get the copper," Alex Rush ordered.

When he returned with the policeman the store detective was waiting in the vestibule.

"Second floor," she said.

Behind her the house's street door stood open to show a dark hallway and the foot of a tattered-carpeted flight of steps. Into this dismal hallway appeared a slovenly thin woman in rumpled gray cotton, saying whiningly as she came forward, "What do you want? I keep a respectable house, I'll have you understand, and I—"

"Chunky, dark-eyed girl living here," Alec Rush croaked. "Second floor. Take us up."

The woman's scrawny face sprang into startled lines, faded eyes wide, as if mistaking the harshness of the detective's voice for the harshness of great emotion.

"Why—why—" she stammered, and then remembered the first principle of shady rooming-house management—never to stand in the way of the police. "I'll take you up," she agreed, and, hitching her wrinkled skirt in one hand, led the way up the stairs.

Her sharp fingers tapped on a door near the head of the stairs.

"Who's that?" a casually curt feminine voice asked.

"Landlady."

The chunky girl in blue, without her hat now, opened the door. Alec Rush moved a big foot forward to hold it open, while the landlady said, "This is her," the policeman said, "You'll have to come along," and Minnie said, "Dearie, we want to come in and talk to you."

"My God!" exclaimed the girl. "There'd be just as much sense to it if you'd all jumped out at me and yelled 'Boo!'"

"This ain't any way," Alec Rush rasped, moving forward, grinning his hideous friendly grin. "Let's go in where we can talk it over."

Merely by moving his loose-jointed bulk a step this way, a half-step that, turning his ugly face on this one and that one, he herded the little group as he wished, sending the landlady discontentedly away, marshaling the others into the girl's rooms.

"Remember, I got no idea what this is all about," said the girl when they were in her living-room, a narrow room where blue fought with red without ever compromising on purple. "I'm easy to get along with, and if you think this is a nice place to talk about whatever you want to talk about, go ahead! But if you're counting on me talking, too, you'd better smart me up."

"Boosting, dearie," Minnie said, leaning forward to pat the girl's arm. "I'm at

Goodbody's."

"You think I've been shoplifting? Is that the idea?"

"Yeah. Exactly. Uh-huh. That's what." Alec Rush left her no doubt on the point.

The girl narrowed her eyes, puckered her red mouth, squinted sidewise at the ugly man.

"It's all right with me," she announced, "so long as Goodbody's hanging the rap on me—somebody I can sue for a million when it flops. I've got nothing to say. Take me for my ride."

"You'll get your ride, sister," the ugly man rasped good-naturedly. "Nobody's going to beat you out of it. But do you mind if I look around your place a little first?"

"Got anything with a judge's name on it that says you can?"

"No."

"Then you don't get a peep!"

Alec Rush chuckled, thrust his hands into his trouser pockets, and began to wander through the rooms, of which there were three. Presently he came out of the bedroom carrying a photograph in a silver frame.

"Who's this?" he asked the girl.

"Try and find out!"

"I am trying," he lied.

"You big bum!" said she. "You couldn't find water in the ocean!"

Alec Rush laughed with coarse heartiness. He could afford to. The photograph in his hand was of Hubert Landow.

Twilight was around the gray stone church when the owner of the deserted coupé returned to it. The chunky girl—Polly Vanness was the name she had given—had been booked and lodged in a cell in the Southwestern Police Station. Quantities of stolen goods had been found in her flat. Her harvest of that afternoon was still on her person when Minnie and a police matron searched her. She had refused to talk. The detective had said nothing to her about his knowledge of the photograph's subject, or of her meeting in the railroad station with the dark young man. Nothing found in her rooms threw any light on either of these things.

Having eaten his evening meal before coming back to his car, Alec Rush now drove out to Charles-Street Avenue. Lights glowed normally in the Landow house when he passed it. A little beyond it he turned his coupé so that it pointed toward the city, and brought it to rest in a tree-darkened curbside spot within sight of the house.

The night went along and no one left or entered the Landow house.

Finger nails clicked on the coupé's glass door.

A man stood there. Nothing could be said of him in the darkness except that he was not large, and that to have escaped the detective's notice until now he must have stealthily stalked the car from the rear.

Alec Rush put out a hand and the door swung open.

"Got a match?" the man asked.

The detective hesitated, said, "Yeah," and held out a box.

A match scraped and flared into a dark young face: large nose, high cheekbones: the young man Alec Rush had shadowed that afternoon.

But recognition, when it was voiced, was voiced by the dark young man.

"I thought it was you," he said simply as he applied the flaming match to his cigarette. "Maybe you don't know me, but I knew you when you were on the force."

The ex-detective-sergeant gave no meaning at all to a husky "Yeah."

"I thought it was you in the heap on Mount Royal this afternoon, but I couldn't make sure," the young man continued, entering the coupé, sitting beside the detective, closing the door. "Scuttle Zeipp's me. I ain't as well known as Napoleon, so if you've never heard of me there's no hard feelings."

"Yeah."

"That's the stuff! When you once think up a good answer, stick to it." Scuttle Zeipp's face was a sudden bronze mask in the glow of his cigarette. "The same answer'll do for my next question. You're interested in these here Landows? Yeah," he added in hoarse mimicry of the detective's voice.

Another inhalation lighted his face, and his words came smokily out as the glow faded.

"You ought to want to know what I'm doing hanging around 'em. I ain't tight. I'll tell you. I've been slipped half a grand to bump off the girl—twice. How do you like that?"

"I hear you," said Alec Rush. "But anybody can talk that knows the words."

"Talk? Sure it's talk," Zeipp admitted cheerfully. "But so's it talk when the judge says 'hanged by the neck until dead and may God have mercy on your soul!' Lots of things are talk, but that don't always keep 'em from being real."

"Yeah?"

"Yeah, brother, yeah! Now listen to this: it's one for the cuff. A certain party comes to me a couple of days ago with a knock-down from a party that knows me. See? This certain party asks me what I want to bump off a broad. I thought a grand would be right, and said so. Too stiff. We come together on five hundred. I got two-fifty down

68

and get the rest when the Landow twist is cold. Not so bad for a soft trick—a slug through the side of a car—huh?"

"Well, what are you waiting for?" the detective asked. "You want to make it a fancy caper—kill her on her birthday or a legal holiday?"

Scuttle Zeipp smacked his lips and poked the detective's chest with a finger in the dark.

"Not any, brother! I'm thinking way ahead of you! Listen to this: I pocket my two-fifty advance and come up here to give the ground a good casing, not wanting to lam into anything I didn't know was here. While I'm poking around, I run into another party that's poking around. This second party gives me a tumble, I talk smart, and bingo! First thing you know she's propositioning me. What do you guess? She wants to know what I want to bump off a broad! Is it the same one *she* wants stopped? I hope to tell you it is!

"I ain't so silly! I get my hands on another two hundred and fifty berries, with that much more coming when I put over the fast one. Now do you think I'm going to do anything to that Landow baby? You're dumb if you do. She's my meal ticket. If she lives till I pop her, she'll be older than either you or the bay. I've got five hundred out of her so far. What's the matter with sticking around and waiting for more customers that don't like her? If two of 'em want to buy her out of the world, why not more? The answer is, 'Yeah!' And on top of that, here you are snooping around her. Now there it is, brother, for you to look at and taste and smell."

Silence held for several minutes, in the darkness of the coupé's interior, and then the detective's harsh voice put a skeptical question:

"And who are these certain parties that want her out of the way?"

"Be yourself!" Scuttle Zeipp admonished him. "I'm laying down on 'em, right enough, but I ain't feeding 'em to you."

"What are you giving me all this for then?"

"What for? Because you're in on the lay somewhere. Crossing each other, neither of us can make a thin dimmer. If we don't hook up we'll just ruin the racket for each other. I've already made half a grand off this Landow. That's mine, but there's more to be picked up by a couple of men that know what they're doing. All right. I'm offering to throw in with you on a two-way cut of whatever else we can get. But my parties are out! I don't mind throwing them down, but I ain't rat enough to put the finger on them for you."

Alec Rush grunted and croaked another dubious inquiry.

"How come you trust me so much, Scuttle?"

The hired killer laughed knowingly.

"Why not? You're a right guy. You can see a profit when it's showed to you. They

69

didn't chuck you off the force for forgetting to hang up your stocking. Besides, suppose you want to double-cross me, what can you do? You can't prove anything. I told you I didn't mean the woman any harm. I ain't even packing a gun. But all that's the bunk. You're a wise head. You know what's what. Me and you, Alec, we can get plenty!"

Silence again, until the detective spoke slowly, thoughtfully.

"The first thing would be to get a line on the reasons your parties want the girl put out. Got anything on that?"

"Not a whisper."

"Both of 'em women, I take it."

Scuttle Zeipp hesitated.

"Yes," he admitted. "But don't be asking me anything about 'em. In the first place, I don't know anything, and in the second, I wouldn't tip their mitts if I did."

"Yeah," the detective croaked, as if he quite understood his companion's perverted idea of loyalty. "Now if they're women, the chances are the racket hangs on a man. What do you think of Landow? He's a pretty lad."

Scuttle Zeipp leaned over to put his finger against the detective's chest again.

"You've got it, Alec! That could be it, damned if it couldn't!"

"Yeah," Alec Rush agreed, fumbling with the levers of his car. "We'll get away from here and stay away until I look into him."

At Franklin Street, half a block from the rooming-house into which he had shadowed the young man that afternoon, the detective stopped his coupé.

"You want to drop out here?" he asked.

Scuttle Zeipp looked sidewise, speculatively, into the elder man's ugly face.

"It'll do," the young man said, "but you're a damned good guesser, just the same." He stopped with a hand on the door. "It's a go, is it, Alec? Fifty-fifty?"

"I wouldn't say so," Alec Rush grinned at him with hideous good-nature. "You're not a bad lad, Scuttle, and if there's any gravy you'll get yours, but don't count on me mobbing up with you."

Zeipp's eyes jerked to slits, his lips snarled back from yellow teeth that were set edge to edge.

"You sell me out, you damned gorilla, and I'll—" He laughed the threat out of being, his dark face young and careless again. "Have it your own way, Alec. I didn't make no mistake when I throwed in with you. What you say goes."

"Yeah," the ugly man agreed. "Lay off that joint out there until I tell you. Maybe

70

you'd better drop in to see me tomorrow. The phone book'll tell you where my office is. So long, kid."

"So long, Alec."

In the morning Alec Rush set about investigating Hubert Landow. First he went to the City Hall, where he examined the gray books in which marriage licenses are indexed. Hubert Britman Landow and Sara Falsoner had been married six months before, he learned.

The bride's maiden name thickened the red in the detective's bloodshot eyes. Air hissed sharply from his flattened nostrils. "Yeah! Yeah!" he said to himself, so raspingly that a lawyer's skinny clerk, fiddling with other records at his elbow, looked frightenedly at him and edged a little away.

From the City Hall, Alec Rush carried the bride's name to two newspaper offices, where, after studying the files, he bought an armful of six-months-old papers. He took the papers to his office, spread them on his desk, and attacked them with a pair of shears. When the last one had been cut and thrown aside, there remained on his desk a thick sheaf of clippings.

Arranging his clippings in chronological order, Alec Rush lighted a black cigar, put his elbows on the desk, his ugly head between his palms, and began to read a story with which newspaper-reading Baltimore had been familiar half a year before.

Purged of irrelevancies and earlier digressions, the story was essentially this:

Jerome Falsoner, aged forty-five, was a bachelor who lived alone in a flat in Cathedral Street, on an income more than sufficient for his comfort. He was a tall man, but of delicate physique, the result, it may have been, of excessive indulgence in pleasure on a constitution none too strong in the beginning. He was well known, at least by sight, to all night-living Baltimoreans, and to those who frequented race-track, gambling-house, and the furtive cockpits that now and then materialize for a few brief hours in the forty miles of country that lie between Baltimore and Washington.

One Fanny Kidd, coming as was her custom at ten o'clock one morning to "do" Jerome Falsoner's rooms, found him lying on his back in his living-room, staring with dead eyes at a spot on the ceiling, a bright spot that was reflected sunlight—reflected from the metal hilt of his paper-knife, which protruded from his chest.

Police investigation established four facts:

First, Jerome Falsoner had been dead for fourteen hours when Fanny Kidd found him, which placed his murder at about eight o'clock the previous evening.

Second, the last persons known to have seen him alive were a woman named Madeline Boudin, with whom he had been intimate, and three of her friends. They had seen him, alive, at some time between seven-thirty and eight o'clock, or less than half an hour before his death. They had been driving down to a cottage on the Severn

River, and Madeline Boudin had told the others she wanted to see Falsoner before she went. The others had remained in their car while she rang the bell. Jerome Falsoner opened the street door and she went in. Ten minutes later she came out and rejoined her friends. Jerome Falsoner came to the door with her, waving a hand at one of the men in the car—a Frederick Stoner, who knew Falsoner slightly, and who was connected with the district attorney's office. Two women, talking on the steps of a house across the street, had also seen Falsoner, and had seen Madeline Boudin and her friends drive away.

Third, Jerome Falsoner's heir and only near relative was his niece, Sara Falsoner, who, by some vagary of chance, was marrying Hubert Landow at the very hour that Fanny Kidd was finding her employer's dead body. Niece and uncle had seldom seen one another. The niece—for police suspicion settled on her for a short space—was definitely proved to have been at home, in her apartment in Carey Street, from six o'clock the evening of the murder until eight-thirty the next morning. Her husband, her fiancé then, had been there with her from six until eleven that evening. Prior to her marriage, the girl had been employed as stenographer by the same trust company that employed Ralph Millar.

Fourth, Jerome Falsoner, who had not the most even of dispositions, had quarreled with an Icelander named Einer Jokumsson in a gambling-house two days before he was murdered. Jokumsson had threatened him. Jokumsson—a short, heavily built man, dark-haired, dark-eyed—had vanished from his hotel, leaving his bags there, the day the body was found, and had not been seen since.

The last of these clippings carefully read, Alec Rush rocked back in his chair and made a thoughtful monster's face at the ceiling. Presently he leaned forward again to look into the telephone directory, and to call the number of Ralph Millar's trust company. But when he got his number he changed his mind.

"Never mind," he said into the instrument, and called a number that was Goodbody's. Minnie, when she came to the telephone, told him that Polly Vanness had been identified as one Polly Bangs, arrested in Milwaukee two years ago for shoplifting, and given a two-year sentence. Minnie also said that Polly Bangs had been released on bail early that morning.

Alec Rush pushed back the telephone and looked through his clippings again until he found the address of Madeline Boudin, the woman who had visited Falsoner so soon before his death. It was a Madison Avenue number. Thither his coupé carried the detective.

No, Miss Boudin did not live there. Yes, she had lived there, but had moved four months ago. Perhaps Mrs. Blender, on the third floor, would know where she lived now. Mrs. Blender did not know. She knew Miss Boudin had moved to an apartment-house in Garrison Avenue, but did not think she was living there now. At the Garrison Avenue house: Miss Boudin had moved away a month and a half ago—somewhere in Mount Royal Avenue, perhaps. The number was not known.

The coupé carried its ugly owner to Mount Royal Avenue, to the apartment building he had seen first Hubert Landow and then Scuttle Zeipp visit the previous day. At the manager's office he made inquiries about a Walter Boyden, who was thought to live there. Walter Boyden was not known to the manager. There was a Miss Boudin in 604, but her name was B-o-u-d-i-n, and she lived alone.

Alec Rush left the building and got in his car again. He screwed up his savage red eyes, nodded his head in a satisfied way, and with one finger described a small circle in the air. Then he returned to his office.

Calling the trust company's number again, he gave Ralph Millar's name, and presently was speaking to the assistant cashier.

"This is Rush. Can you come up to the office right away?"

"What's that? Certainly. But how—how—? Yes, I'll be up in a minute."

None of the surprise that had been in Millar's telephone voice was apparent when he reached the detective's office. He asked no questions concerning the detective's knowledge of his identity. In brown today, he was as neatly inconspicuous as he had been yesterday in gray.

"Come in," the ugly man welcomed him. "Sit down. I've got to have some more facts, Mr. Millar."

Millar's thin mouth tightened and his brows drew together with obstinate reticence.

"I thought we settled that point, Rush. I told you——"

Alec Rush frowned at his client with jovial, though frightful exasperation.

"I know what you told me," he interrupted. "But that was then and this is now. The thing's coming unwound on me, and I can see just enough to get myself tangled up if I don't watch Harvey. I found your mysterious man, talked to him. He was following Mrs. Landow, right enough. According to the way he tells it, he's been hired to kill her."

Millar leaped from his chair to lean over the yellow desk, his face close to the detective's.

"My God, Rush, what are you saying? To kill her?"

"Now, now! Take it easy. He's not going to kill her. I don't think he ever meant to. But he claims he was hired to do it."

"You've arrested him? You've found the man who hired him?"

The detective squinted up his bloodshot eyes and studied the younger man's passionate face.

"As a matter of fact," he croaked calmly when he had finished his examination, "I haven't done either of those things. She's in no danger just now. Maybe the lad was

73

stringing me, maybe he wasn't, but either way he wouldn't have spilled it to me if he meant to do anything. And when it comes right down to it, Mr. Millar, do you want him arrested?"

"Yes! That is——" Millar stepped back from the desk, sagged limply down on the chair again, and put shaking hands over his face. "My God, Rush, I don't know!" he gasped.

"Exactly," said Alec Rush. "Now here it is. Mrs. Landow was Jerome Falsoner's niece and heir. She worked for your trust company. She married Landow the morning her uncle was found dead. Yesterday Landow visited the building where Madeline Boudin lives. She was the last person known to have been in Falsoner's rooms before he was killed. But her alibi seems to be as air-tight as the Landows'. The man who claims he was hired to kill Mrs. Landow also visited Madeline Boudin's building yesterday. I saw him go in. I saw him meet another woman. A shoplifter, the second one. In her rooms I found a photograph of Hubert Landow. Your dark man claims he was hired twice to kill Mrs. Landow—by two women neither knowing the other had hired him. He won't tell me who they are, but he doesn't have to."

The hoarse voice stopped and Alec Rush waited for Millar to speak. But Millar was for the time without a voice. His eyes were wide and despairingly empty. Alec Rush raised one big hand, folded it into a fist that was almost perfectly spherical, and thumped his desk softly.

"There it is, Mr. Millar," he rasped. "A pretty tangle. If you'll tell me what you know, we'll get it straightened out, never fear. If you don't—I'm out!"

Now Millar found words, however jumbled.

"You couldn't, Rush! You can't desert me—us—her! It's not—You're not——"

But Alec Rush shook his ugly pear-shaped head with slow emphasis.

"There's murder in this and the Lord knows what all. I've got no liking for a blindfolded game. How do I know what you're up to? You can tell me what you know —everything—or you can find yourself another detective. That's flat."

Ralph Millar's fingers picked at each other, his teeth pulled at his lips, his harassed eyes pleaded with the detective.

"You can't, Rush," he begged. "She's still in danger. Even if you are right about that man not attacking her, she's not safe. The women who hired him can hire another. You've got to protect her, Rush."

"Yeah? Then you've got to talk."

"I've got to—? Yes, I'll talk, Rush. I'll tell you anything you ask. But there's really nothing—or almost nothing—I know beyond what you've already learned."

"She worked for your trust company?"

74

"Yes, in my department."

"Left there to be married?"

"Yes. That is—No, Rush, the truth is she was discharged. It was an outrage, but——"

"When was this?"

"It was the day before the—before she was married."

"Tell me about it."

"She had—I'll have to explain her situation to you first, Rush. She is an orphan. Her father, Ben Falsoner, had been wild in his youth—and perhaps not only in his youth —as I believe all the Falsoners have been. However, he had quarreled with his father —old Howard Falsoner—and the old man had cut him out of the will. But not altogether out. The old man hoped Ben would mend his ways, and he didn't mean to leave him with nothing in that event. Unfortunately he trusted it to his other son, Jerome.

"Old Howard Falsoner left a will whereby the income from his estate was to go to Jerome during Jerome's life. Jerome was to provide for his brother Ben as he saw fit. That is, he had an absolutely free hand. He could divide the income equally with his brother, or he could give him a pittance, or he could give him nothing, as Ben's conduct deserved. On Jerome's death the estate was to be divided equally among the old man's grandchildren.

"In theory, that was a fairly sensible arrangement, but not in practice—not in Jerome Falsoner's hands. You didn't know him? Well, he was the last man you'd ever trust with a thing of that sort. He exercised his power to the utmost. Ben Falsoner never got a cent from him. Three years ago Ben died, and so the girl, his only daughter, stepped into his position in relation to her grandfather's money. Her mother was already dead. Jerome Falsoner never paid her a cent.

"That was her situation when she came to the trust company two years ago. It wasn't a happy one. She had at least a touch of the Falsoner recklessness and extravagance. There she was: heiress to some two million dollars—for Jerome had never married and she was the only grandchild—but without any present income at all, except her salary, which was by no means a large one.

"She got in debt. I suppose she tried to economize at times, but there was always that two million dollars ahead to make scrimping doubly distasteful. Finally, the trust company officials heard of her indebtedness. A collector or two came to the office, in fact. Since she was employed in my department, I had the disagreeable duty of warning her. She promised to pay her debts and contract no more, and I suppose she did try, but she wasn't very successful. Our officials are old-fashioned, ultra-conservative. I did everything I could to save her, but it was no good. They simply would not have an employee who was heels over head in debt."

Millar paused a moment, looked miserably at the floor, and went on:

75

"I had the disagreeable task of telling her her services were no longer needed. I tried to—It was awfully unpleasant. That was the day before she married Landow. It—" he paused and, as if he could think of nothing else to say, repeated, "Yes, it was the day before she married Landow," and fell to staring miserably at the floor again.

Alec Rush, who had sat as still through the recital of this history as a carven monster on an old church, now leaned over his desk and put a husky question:

"And who is this Hubert Landow? What is he?"

Ralph Millar shook his downcast head.

"I don't know him. I've seen him. I know nothing of him."

"Mrs. Landow ever speak of him? I mean when she was in the trust company?"

"It's likely, but I don't remember."

"So you didn't know what to make of it when you heard she'd married him?"

The younger man looked up with frightened brown eyes.

"What are you getting at, Rush? You don't think—Yes, as you say, I was surprised. What are you getting at?"

"The marriage license," the detective said, ignoring his client's repeated question, "was issued to Landow four days before the wedding-day, four days before Jerome Falsoner's body was found."

Millar chewed a finger nail and shook his head hopelessly.

"I don't know what you're getting at," he mumbled around the finger. "The whole thing is bewildering."

"Isn't it a fact, Mr. Millar," the detective's voice filled the office with hoarse insistence, "that you were on more friendly terms with Sara Falsoner than with anyone else in the trust company?"

The younger man raised his head and looked Alec Rush in the eye—held his gaze with brown eyes that were doggedly level.

"The fact is," he said quietly, "that I asked Sara Falsoner to marry me the day she left."

"Yeah. And she——?"

"And she—I suppose it was my fault. I was clumsy, crude, whatever you like. God knows what she thought—that I was asking her to marry me out of pity, that I was trying to force her into marriage by discharging her when I knew she was over her head in debt! She might have thought anything. Anyhow, it was—it was disagreeable."

"You mean she not only refused you, but was—well—disagreeable about it?"

76

"I do mean that."

Alec Rush sat back in his chair and brought fresh grotesqueries into his face by twisting his thick mouth crookedly up at one corner. His red eyes were evilly reflective on the ceiling.

"The only thing for it," he decided, "is to go to Landow and give him what we've got."

"But are you sure he—?" Millar objected indefinitely.

"Unless he's one whale of an actor, he's a lot in love with his wife," the detective said with certainty. "That's enough to justify taking the story to him."

Millar was not convinced.

"You're sure it would be wisest?"

"Yeah. We've got to go to one of three people with the tale—him, her, or the police. I think he's the best bet, but take your choice."

The younger man nodded reluctantly.

"All right. But you don't have to bring me into it, do you?" with quick alarm. "You can handle it so I won't be involved. You understand what I mean? She's his wife, and it would be——"

"Sure," Alec Rush promised, "I'll keep you covered up."

Hubert Landow, twisting the detective's card in his fingers, received Alec Rush in a somewhat luxuriously furnished room in the second story of the Charles-Street Avenue house. He was standing—tall, blond, boyishly handsome—in the middle of the floor, facing the door, when the detective—fat, grizzled, battered and ugly—was shown in.

"You wish to see me? Here, sit down."

Hubert Landow's manner was neither restrained nor hearty. It was precisely the manner that might be expected of a young man receiving an unexpected call from so savage-visaged a detective.

"Yeah," said Alec Rush as they sat in facing chairs. "I've got something to tell you. It won't take much time, but it's kind of wild. It might be a surprise to you, and it might not. But it's on the level. I don't want you to think I'm kidding you."

Hubert Landow bent forward, his face all interest.

"I won't," he promised. "Go on."

"A couple of days ago I got a line on a man who might be tied up in a job I'm interested in. He's a crook. Trailing him around, I discovered he was interested in your affairs, and your wife's. He's shadowed you and he's shadowed her. He was loafing down the street from a Mount Royal Avenue apartment that you went in

77

yesterday, and he went in there later himself."

"But what the devil is he up to?" Landow exclaimed. "You think he's——"

"Wait," the ugly man advised. "Wait until you've heard it all, and then you can tell me what you make of it. He came out of there and went to Camden Station, where he met a young woman. They talked a bit, and later in the afternoon she was picked up in a department store—shoplifting. Her name is Polly Bangs, and she's done a hitch in Wisconsin for the same racket. Your photograph was on her dresser."

"My photograph?"

Alec Rush nodded placidly up into the face of the young man who was now standing.

"Yours. You know this Polly Bangs? A chunky, square-built girl of twenty-six or so, with brown hair and eyes—saucy looking?"

Hubert Landow's face was a puzzled blank.

"No! What the devil could she be doing with my picture?" he demanded. "Are you sure it was mine?"

"Not dead sure, maybe, but sure enough to need proof that it wasn't. Maybe she's somebody you've forgotten, or maybe she ran across the picture somewhere and kept it because she liked it."

"Nonsense!" The blond man squirmed at this tribute to his face, and blushed a vivid red beside which Alec Rush's complexion was almost colorless. "There must be some sensible reason. She has been arrested, you say?"

"Yeah, but she's out on bail now. But let me get along with my story. Last night this thug I've told you about and I had a talk. He claims he has been hired to kill your wife."

Hubert Landow, who had returned to his chair, now jerked in it so that its joints creaked strainingly. His face, crimson a second ago, drained paperwhite. Another sound than the chair's creaking was faint in the room: the least of muffled gasps. The blond young man did not seem to hear it, but Alec Rush's bloodshot eyes flicked sidewise for an instant to focus fleetingly on a closed door across the room.

Landow was out of his chair again, leaning down to the detective, his fingers digging into the ugly man's loose muscular shoulders.

"This is horrible!" he was crying. "We've got to—"

The door at which the detective had looked a moment ago opened. A beautiful tall girl came through—Sara Landow. Her hair rumpled, was an auburn cloud around her white face. Her eyes were dead things. She walked slowly toward the men, her body inclined a little forward, as if against a strong wind.

"It's no use, Hubert." Her voice was dead as her eyes. "We may as well face it. It's Madeline Boudin. She has found out that I killed my uncle."

78

"Hush, darling, hush!" Landow caught his wife in his arms and tried to soothe her with a caressing hand on her shoulder. "You don't know what you're saying."

"Oh, but I do." She shrugged herself listlessly out of his arms and sat in the chair Alec Rush had just vacated. "It's Madeline Boudin, you know it is. She knows I killed Uncle Jerome."

Landow whirled to the detective, both hands going out to grip the ugly man's arm.

"You won't listen to what she's saying, Rush?" he pleaded. "She hasn't been well. She doesn't know what she's saying."

Sara Landow laughed with weary bitterness.

"Haven't been well?" she said. "No, I haven't been well, not since I killed him. How could I be well after that? You are a detective." Her eyes lifted their emptiness to Alec Rush. "Arrest me. I killed Jerome Falsoner."

Alec Rush, standing arms akimbo, legs apart, scowled at her, saying nothing.

"You can't, Rush!" Landow was tugging at the detective's arm again. "You can't, man. It's ridiculous! You—"

"Where does this Madeline Boudin fit in?" Alec Rush's harsh voice demanded. "I know she was chummy with Jerome, but why should she want your wife killed?"

Landow hesitated, shifting his feet, and when he replied it was reluctantly.

"She was Jerome's mistress, had a child by him. My wife, when she learned of it, insisted on making her a settlement out of the estate. It was in connection with that that I went to see her yesterday."

"Yeah. Now to get back to Jerome: you and your wife were supposed to be in her apartment at the time he was killed, if I remember right?"

Sara Landow sighed with spiritless impatience.

"Must there be all this discussion?" she asked in a small, tired voice. "I killed him. No one else killed him. No one else was there when I killed him. I stabbed him with the paper-knife when he attacked me, and he said, 'Don't! Don't!' and began to cry, down on his knees, and I ran out."

Alec Rush looked from the girl to the man. Landow's face was wet with perspiration, his hands were white fists, and something quivered in his chest. When he spoke his voice was as hoarse as the detective's, if not so loud.

"Sara, will you wait here until I come back? I'm going out for a little while, possibly an hour. You'll wait here and not do anything until I return?"

"Yes," the girl said, neither curiosity nor interest in her voice. "But it's no use, Hubert. I should have told you in the beginning. It's no use."

"Just wait for me, Sara," he pleaded, and then bent his head to the detective's deformed ear. "Stay with her, Rush, for God's sake!" he whispered, and went swiftly out of the room.

The front door banged shut. An automobile purred away from the house. Alec Rush spoke to the girl.

"Where's the phone?"

"In the next room," she said, without looking up from the handkerchief her fingers were measuring.

The detective crossed to the door through which she had entered the room, found that it opened into a library, where a telephone stood in a corner. On the other side of the room a clock indicated three-thirty-five. The detective went to the telephone and called Ralph Millar's office, asked for Millar, and told him:

"This is Rush. I'm at the Landows'. Come up right away."

"But I can't, Rush. Can't you understand my—"

"Can't hell!" croaked Alec Rush. "Get here quick!"

The young woman with dead eyes, still playing with the hem of her handkerchief, did not look up when the ugly man returned to the room. Neither of them spoke. Alec Rush, standing with his back to a window, twice took out his watch to glare savagely at it.

The faint tingling of the doorbell came from below. The detective went across to the hall door and down the front stairs, moving with heavy swiftness. Ralph Millar, his face a field in which fear and embarrassment fought, stood in the vestibule, stammering something unintelligible to the maid who had opened the door. Alec Rush put the girl brusquely aside, brought Millar in, guided him upstairs.

"She says she killed Jerome," he muttered into his client's ear as they mounted.

Ralph Millar's face went dreadfully white, but there was no surprise in it.

"You knew she killed him?" Alec Rush growled.

Millar tried twice to speak and made no sound. They were on the second-floor landing before the words came.

"I saw her on the street that night, going toward his flat!"

Alec Rush snorted viciously and turned the younger man toward the room where Sara Landow sat.

"Landow's out," he whispered hurriedly. "I'm going out. Stay with her. She's shot to hell—likely to do anything if she's left alone. If Landow gets back before I do, tell him to wait for me."

Before Millar could voice the confusion in his face they were across the sill and into the room. Sara Landow raised her head. Her body was lifted from the chair as if by

80

an invisible power. She came up tall and erect on her feet. Millar stood just inside the door. They looked eye into eye, posed each as if in the grip of a force pushing them together, another holding them apart.

Alec Rush hurried clumsily and silently down to the street.

In Mount Royal Avenue, Alec Rush saw the blue roadster at once. It was standing empty before the apartment building in which Madeline Boudin lived. The detective drove past it and turned his coupé in to the curb three blocks below. He had barely come to rest there when Landow ran out of the apartment building, jumped into his car, and drove off. He drove to a Charles Street hotel. Behind him went the detective.

In the hotel, Landow walked straight to the writing room. For half an hour he sat there, bending over a desk, covering sheet after sheet of paper with rapidly written words, while the detective sat behind a newspaper in a secluded angle of the lobby, watching the writing-room exit. Landow came out of the room stuffing a thick envelope in his pocket, left the hotel, got into his machine, and drove to the office of a messenger service company in St. Paul Street.

He remained in this office for five minutes. When he came out he ignored his roadster at the curb, walking instead to Calvert Street, where he boarded a northbound street-car. Alec Rush's coupé rolled along behind the car. At Union Station, Landow left the street-car and went to the ticket window. He had just asked for a one-way ticket to Philadelphia when Alec Rush tapped him on the shoulder.

Hubert Landow turned slowly, the money for his ticket still in his hand. Recognition brought no expression to his handsome face.

"Yes," he said coolly, "what is it?"

Alec Rush nodded his ugly head at the ticket-window, at the money in Landow's hand.

"This is nothing for you to be doing," he growled.

"Here you are," the ticket-seller said through his grille. Neither of the men in front paid any attention to him. A large woman in pink, red and violet, jostling Landow, stepped on his foot and pushed past him to the window. Landow stepped back, the detective following.

"You shouldn't have left Sara alone," said Landow. "She's—"

"She's not alone. I got somebody to stay with her."

"Not—?"

"Not the police, if that's what you're thinking."

Landow began to pace slowly down the long concourse, the detective keeping step with him. The blond man stopped and looked sharply into the other's face.

"Is it that fellow Millar who's with her?" he demanded.

81

"Yeah."

"Is he the man you're working for, Rush?"

"Yeah."

Landow resumed his walking. When they had reached the northern extremity of the concourse, he spoke again.

"What does he want, this Millar?"

Alec Rush shrugged his thick, limber shoulders and said nothing.

"Well, what do you want?" the young man asked with some heat, facing the detective squarely now.

"I don't want you going out of town."

Landow pondered that, scowling.

"Suppose I insist on going," he asked, "how will you stop me?"

"Accomplice after the fact in Jerome's murder would be a charge I could hold you on."

Silence again, until broken by Landow.

"Look here, Rush. You're working for Millar. He's out at my house. I've just sent a letter out to Sara by messenger. Give them time to read it, and then phone Millar there. Ask him if he wants me held or not."

Alec Rush shook his head decidedly.

"No good," he rasped. "Millar's too rattle-brained for me to take his word for anything like that over the phone. We'll go back there and have a talk all around."

Now it was Landow who balked.

"No," he snapped. "I won't!" He looked with cool calculation at the detective's ugly face. "Can I buy you, Rush?"

"No, Landow. Don't let my looks and my record kid you."

"I thought not." Landow looked at the roof and at his feet, and he blew his breath out sharply. "We can't talk here. Let's find a quiet place."

"The heap's outside," Alec Rush said, "and we can sit in that."

Seated in Alec Rush's coupé, Hubert Landow lighted a cigarette, the detective one of his black cigars.

"That Polly Bangs you were talking about, Rush," the blond man said without preamble, "is my wife. My name is Henry Bangs. You won't find my fingerprints anywhere. When Polly was picked up in Milwaukee a couple of years ago and sent over, I came east and fell in with Madeline Boudin. We made a good team. She had

82

brains in chunks, and if I've got somebody to do my thinking for me, I'm a pretty good worker myself."

He smiled at the detective, pointing at his own face with his cigarette. While Alec Rush watched, a tide of crimson surged into the blond man's face until it was rosy as a blushing school-girl's. He laughed again and the blush began to fade.

"That's my best trick," he went on. "Easy if you have the gift and keep in practice: fill your lungs, try to force the air out while keeping it shut off at the larynx. It's a gold mine for a grifter! You'd be surprised how people will trust me after I've turned on a blush or two for 'em. So Madeline and I were in the money. She had brains, nerve and a good front. I have everything but brains. We turned a couple of tricks—one con and one blackmail—and then she ran into Jerome Falsoner. We were going to give him the squeeze at first. But when Madeline found out that Sara was his heiress, that she was in debt, and that she and her uncle were on the outs, we ditched that racket and cooked a juicier one. Madeline found somebody to introduce me to Sara. I made myself agreeable, playing the boob—the shy but worshipful young man.

"Madeline had brains, as I've said. She used 'em all this time. I hung around Sara, sending her candy, books, flowers, taking her to shows and dinner. The books and shows were part of Madeline's work. Two of the books mentioned the fact that a husband can't be made to testify against his wife in court, nor wife against husband. One of the plays touched the same thing. That was planting the seeds. We planted another with my blushing and mumbling—persuaded Sara, or rather let her discover for herself, that I was the clumsiest liar in the world.

"The planting done, we began to push the game along. Madeline kept on good terms with Jerome. Sara was getting deeper in debt. We helped her in still deeper. We had a burglar clean out her apartment one night—Ruby Sweeger, maybe you know him. He's in stir now for another caper. He got what money she had and most of the things she could have hocked in a pinch. Then we stirred up some of the people she owed, sent them anonymous letters warning them not to count too much on her being Jerome's heir. Foolish letters, but they did the trick. A couple of her creditors sent collectors to the trust company.

"Jerome got his income from the estate quarterly. Madeline knew the dates, and Sara knew them. The day before the next one, Madeline got busy on Sara's creditors again. I don't know what she told them this time, but it was enough. They descended on the trust company in a flock, with the result that the next day Sara was given two weeks' pay and discharged. When she came out I met her—by chance—yes, I'd been watching for her since morning. I took her for a drive and got her back to her apartment at six o'clock. There we found more frantic creditors waiting to pounce on her. I chased them out, played the big-hearted boy, making embarrassed offers of all sorts of help. She refused them, of course, and I could see decision coming into her face. She knew this was the day on which Jerome got his quarterly check. She determined to go see him, to demand that he pay her debts at least. She didn't tell me where she was going, but I could see it plain enough, since I was looking for it.

"I left her and waited across the street from her apartment, in Franklin Square, until I saw her come out. Then I found a telephone, called up Madeline, and told her Sara was on her way to her uncle's flat."

Landow's cigarette scorched his fingers. He dropped it, crushed it under his foot, lighted another.

"This is a long-winded story, Rush," he apologized, "but it'll soon be over now."

"Keep talking, son," said Alec Rush.

"There were some people in Madeline's place when I phoned her—people trying to persuade her to go down the country on a party. She agreed now. They would give her an even better alibi than the one she had cooked up. She told them she had to see Jerome before she left, and they drove her over to his place and waited in their car while she went in with him.

"She had a pint bottle of cognac with her, all doped and ready. She poured out a drink of it for Jerome, telling him of the new bootlegger she had found who had a dozen or more cases of this cognac to sell at a reasonable price. The cognac was good enough and the price low enough to make Jerome think she had dropped in to let him in on something good. He gave her an order to pass on to the bootlegger. Making sure his steel paper-knife was in full view on the table, Madeline rejoined her friends, taking Jerome as far as the door so they would see he was still alive, and drove off.

"Now I don't know what Madeline had put in that cognac. If she told me, I've forgotten. It was a powerful drug—not a poison, you understand, but an excitant. You'll see what I mean when you hear the rest. Sara must have reached her uncle's flat ten or fifteen minutes after Madeline's departure. Her uncle's face, she says, was red, inflamed, when he opened the door for her. But he was a frail man, while she was strong, and she wasn't afraid of the devil himself, for that matter. She went in and demanded that he settle her debts, even if he didn't choose to make her an allowance out of his income.

"They were both Falsoners, and the argument must have grown hot. Also the drug was working on Jerome, and he had no will with which to fight it. He attacked her. The paper-knife was on the table, as Madeline had seen. He was a maniac. Sara was not one of your corner-huddling, screaming girls. She grabbed the paper-knife and let him have it. When he fell, she turned and ran.

"Having followed her as soon as I'd finished telephoning to Madeline, I was standing on Jerome's front steps when she dashed out. I stopped her and she told me she'd killed her uncle. I made her wait there while I went in, to see if he was really dead. Then I took her home, explaining my presence at Jerome's door by saying, in my boobish, awkward way, that I had been afraid she might do something reckless and had thought it best to keep an eye on her.

"Back in her apartment, she was all for giving herself up to the police. I pointed out the danger in that, arguing that, in debt, admittedly going to her uncle for money, being his heiress, she would most certainly be convicted of having murdered him so she would get the money. Her story of his attack, I persuaded her, would be laughed at as a flimsy yarn. Dazed, she wasn't hard to convince. The next step was easy. The police would investigate her, even if they didn't especially suspect her. I was, so far as we knew, the only person whose testimony could convict her. I was loyal enough, but wasn't I the clumsiest liar in the world? Didn't the mildest lie make me blush like an auctioneer's flag? The way around that difficulty lay in what two of the books I had given her, and one of the plays we had seen, had shown: if I was her husband I couldn't be made to testify against her. We were married the next morning, on a license I had been carrying for nearly a week.

"Well, there we were. I was married to her. She had a couple of millions coming when her uncle's affairs were straightened out. She couldn't possibly, it seemed, escape arrest and conviction. Even if no one had seen her entering or leaving her uncle's flat, everything still pointed to her guilt, and the foolish course I had persuaded her to follow would simply ruin her chance of pleading self-defense. If they hanged her, the two million would come to me. If she got a long term in prison, I'd have the handling of the money at least."

Landow dropped and crushed his second cigarette and stared for a moment straight ahead into distance.

"Do you believe in God, or Providence, or Fate, or any of that, Rush?" he asked. "Well, some believe in one thing and some in another, but listen. Sara was never arrested, never even really suspected. It seems there was some sort of Finn or Swede who had had a run-in with Jerome and threatened him. I suppose he couldn't account for his whereabouts the night of the killing, so he went into hiding when he heard of Jerome's murder. The police suspicion settled on him. They looked Sara up, of course, but not very thoroughly. No one seems to have seen her in the street, and the people in her apartment house, having seen her come in at six o'clock with me, and not having seen her—or not remembering if they did—go out or in again, told the police she had been in all evening. The police were too much interested in the missing Finn, or whatever he was, to look any further into Sara's affairs.

"So there we were again. I was married into the money, but I wasn't fixed so I could hand Madeline her cut. Madeline said we'd let things run along as they were until the estate was settled up, and then we could tip Sara off to the police. But by the time the money was settled up there was another hitch. This one was my doing. I—I—well, I wanted to go on just as we were. Conscience had nothing to do with it, you understand? It was simply that—well—that living on with Sara was the only thing I wanted. I wasn't even sorry for what I'd done, because if it hadn't been for that I would never have had her.

"I don't know whether I can make this clear to you, Rush, but even now I don't regret any of it. If it could have been different—but it couldn't. It had to be this way or none. And I've had those six months. I can see that I've been a chump. Sara was never for me. I got her by a crime and a trick, and while I held on to a silly hope that

85

some day she'd—she'd look at me as I did at her, I knew in my heart all the time it was no use. There had been a man—your Millar. She's free now that it's out about my being married to Polly, and I hope she—I hope—Well, Madeline began to howl for action. I told Sara that Madeline had had a child by Jerome, and Sara agreed to settle some money on her. But that didn't satisfy Madeline. It wasn't sentiment with her. I mean, it wasn't any feeling for me, it was just the money. She wanted every cent she could get, and she couldn't get enough to satisfy her in a settlement of the kind Sara wanted to make.

"With Polly, it was that too, but maybe a little more. She's fond of me, I think. I don't know how she traced me here after she got out of the Wisconsin big house, but I can see how she figured things. I was married to a wealthy woman. If the woman died—shot by a bandit in a hold-up attempt—then I'd have money, and Polly would have both me and money. I haven't seen her, wouldn't know she was in Baltimore if you hadn't told me, but that's the way it would work out in her mind. The killing idea would have occurred just as easily to Madeline. I had told her I wouldn't stand for pushing the game through on Sara. Madeline knew that if she went ahead on her own hook and hung the Falsoner murder on Sara I'd blow up the whole racket. But if Sara died, then I'd have the money and Madeline would draw her cut. So that was it.

"I didn't know that until you told me, Rush. I don't give a damn for your opinion of me, but it's God's truth that I didn't know that either Polly or Madeline was trying to have Sara killed. Well, that's about all. Were you shadowing me when I went to the hotel?"

"Yeah."

"I thought so. That letter I wrote and sent home told just about what I've told you, spilled the whole story. I was going to run for it, leaving Sara in the clear. She's clear, all right, but now I'll have to face it. But I don't want to see her again, Rush."

"I wouldn't think you would," the detective agreed. "Not after making a killer of her."

"But I didn't," Landow protested. "She isn't. I forgot to tell you that, but I put it in the letter. Jerome Falsoner was not dead, not even dying, when I went past her into the flat. The knife was too high in his chest. I killed him, driving the knife into the same wound again, but downward. That's what I went in for, to make sure he was finished!"

Alec Rush screwed up his savage bloodshot eyes, looked long into the confessed murderer's face.

"That's a lie," he croaked at last, "but a decent one. Are you sure you want to stick to it? The truth will be enough to clear the girl, and maybe won't swing you."

"What difference does it make?" the younger man asked "I'm a gone baby anyhow. And I might as well put Sara in the clear with herself as well as with the law. I'm caught to rights and another rap won't hurt. I told you Madeline had brains. I was afraid of them. She'd have had something up her sleeve to spring on us—to ruin Sara with. She could out-smart me without trying. I couldn't take any chances."

He laughed into Alec Rush's ugly face and, with a somewhat theatrical gesture, jerked one cuff an inch or two out of his coat-sleeve. The cuff was still damp with a maroon stain.

"I killed Madeline an hour ago," said Henry Bangs, alias Hubert Landow.

NIGHT SHADE

A sedan with no lights burning was standing beside the road just above Piney Falls bridge and as I drove past it a girl put her head out and said, "Please." Her voice was urgent but there was not enough excitement in it to make it either harsh or shrill.

I put on my brakes, then backed up. By that time a man had got out of the sedan. There was enough light to let me see he was young and fairly big. He moved a hand in the direction I had been going and said, "On your way, buddy."

The girl said again, "Will you drive me into town, please?" She seemed to be trying to open the sedan door. Her hat had been pushed forward over one eye.

I said, "Sure."

The man in the road took a step toward me, moved his hand as before, and growled, "Scram, you."

I got out of my car. The man in the road had started toward me when another man's voice came from the sedan, a harsh warning voice. "Go easy, Tony. It's Jack Bye." The sedan door swung open and the girl jumped out.

Tony said, "Oh!" and his feet shuffled uncertainly on the road; but when he saw the girl making for my car he cried indignantly at her, "Listen, you can't ride to town with—"

She was in my roadster by then. "Good night," she said.

He faced me, shook his head stubbornly, began, "I'll be damned if I'll let—"

I hit him. The knock-down was fair enough, because I hit him hard, but I think he could have got up again if he had wanted to. I gave him a little time, then asked the fellow in the sedan, "All right with you?" I still could not see him.

"He'll be all right," he replied quickly. "I'll take care of him all right."

"Thanks." I climbed into my car beside the girl. The rain I had been trying to get to town ahead of was beginning to fall. A coupé with a man and a woman in it passed us going toward town. We followed the coupé across the bridge.

The girl said, "This is awfully kind of you. I wasn't in any danger back there, but it

87

was—nasty."

"They wouldn't be dangerous," I said, "but they would be—nasty."

"You know them?"

"No."

"But they knew you. Tony Forrest and Fred Barnes." When I did not say anything, she added, "They were afraid of you."

"I'm a desperate character."

She laughed. "And pretty nice of you, too, tonight. I wouldn't've gone with either of them alone, but I thought with two of them ..." She turned up the collar of her coat. "It's raining in on me."

I stopped the roadster again and hunted for the curtain that belonged on her side of the car. "So your name's Jack Bye," she said while I was snapping it on.

"And yours is Helen Warner."

"How'd you know?" She had straightened her hat.

"I've seen you around." I finished attaching the curtain and got back in.

"Did you know who I was when I called to you?" she asked when we were moving again.

"Yes."

"It was silly of me to go out with them like that."

"You're shivering."

"It's chilly."

I said I was sorry my flask was empty.

We had turned into the western end of Hellman Avenue. It was four minutes past ten by the clock in front of the jewelry store on the corner of Laurel Street. A policeman in a black rubber coat was leaning against the clock. I did not know enough about perfumes to know the name of hers.

She said, "I'm chilly. Can't we stop somewhere and get a drink?"

"Do you really want to?" My voice must have puzzled her; she turned her head quickly to peer at me in the dim light.

"I'd like to," she said, "unless you're in a hurry."

"No. We could go to Mack's. It's only three or four blocks from here, but—it's a nigger joint."

She laughed. "All I ask is that I don't get poisoned."

88

"You won't, but you're sure you want to go?"

"Certainly." She exaggerated her shivering. "I'm cold. It's early."

Toots Mack opened his door for us. I could tell by the politeness with which he bowed his round bald black head and said, "Good evening, sir; good evening, madam," that he wished we had gone some place else, but I was not especially interested in how he felt about it. I said, "Hello, Toots; how are you this evening?" too cheerfully.

There were only a few customers in the place. We went to the table in the corner farthest from the piano. Suddenly she was staring at me, her eyes, already very blue, becoming very round.

"I thought you could see in the car," I began.

"How'd you get that scar?" she asked, interrupting me. She sat down.

"That." I put a hand to my cheek. "Fight—couple of years ago. You ought to see the one on my chest."

"We'll have to go swimming some time," she said gayly.

"Please sit down and don't keep me waiting for my drink."

"Are you sure you—"

She began to chant, keeping time with her fingers on the table, "I want a drink, I want a drink, I want a drink." Her mouth was small with full lips and it curved up without growing wider when she smiled.

We ordered drinks. We talked too fast. We made jokes and laughed too readily at them. We asked questions—about the name of the perfume she used was one—and paid too much or no attention to the answers. And Toots looked glumly at us from behind the bar when he thought we were not looking at him. It was all pretty bad. We had another drink and I said, "Well, let's slide along."

She was nice about seeming neither too anxious to go nor to stay. The ends of her pale blonde hair curled up over the edge of her hat in back.

At the door I said, "Listen, there's a taxi-stand around the corner. You won't mind if I don't take you home?"

She put a hand on my arm. "I do mind. Please—" The street was badly lighted. Her face was like a child's. She took her hand off my arm. "But if you'd rather ..."

"I think I'd rather."

She said slowly, "I like you, Jack Bye, and I'm awfully grateful for—"

I said, "Aw, that's all right," and we shook hands and I went back into the speakeasy.

Toots was still behind the bar. He came up to where I stood. "You oughtn't to do that

89

to me," he said, shaking his head mournfully.

"I know. I'm sorry."

"You oughtn't to do it to yourself," he went on just as sadly. "This ain't Harlem, boy, and if old Judge Warner finds out his daughter's running around with you and coming in here he can make it plenty tough for both of us. I like you, boy, but you got to remember it don't make no difference how light your skin is or how many colleges you went to, you're still nigger."

I said, "Well, what do you suppose I want to be? A Chinaman?"

THE JUDGE LAUGHED LAST

"The trouble with this country," Old Man Covey unexpectedly exploded, emphasizing his words with repeated beats of a gnarled forefinger on the newspaper he had been reading, "is that the courts have got a stranglehold on it! Law? There ain't no law! There's courts and there's judges, and this thing you call the law is a weapon they use to choke human enterprise—to discourage originality and progress!"

The portion of the morning paper upon which the old man's assault was concentrated, I saw with difficulty, held the report of a decision of the Supreme Court in connection with some labor difficulties in the West. Old Man Covey, I knew, couldn't be personally interested in either side of the dispute. He had as little to do with capital as with labor, which was very little. For eight years now—since the day when a street preacher had turned "Big-dog" Covey from the ways of crime, to become plain John Covey and, later, Old Man Covey—he had subsisted upon the benevolence of a son-in-law.

His interest in this case was, then, purely academic. But his attitude was undoubtedly tinged by his earlier experience with the criminal courts, which had been more than superficial, and I suspected that some especially bitter memory had engendered this outburst.

So I rolled another cigarette and led him gently along the road of argumentation—the most direct path, I had learned, to the interior of his contrary old mind.

"Being a beak," I said, using the vernacular term for judge in an attempt to do all I could to stir up the portions of his remembrance that had to do with his days of youth and lawlessness, "is a tough job. Laws are complicated and puzzling, and it isn't easy to straighten them out so that they fit particular cases. Most of the beaks do very well, I think."

"You think so, do you?" the old scoundrel snarled at me. "Well, let me tell you, sonny, you don't know a damned thing about it! I could tell you stories about beaks

90

and their ways that would knock your eye out!"

I put all the skepticism I could summon into a smile, confident now that I had him.

"You look at things from your own side," I replied, "and in those days you were on the wrong side. Now I don't say that judges don't make mistakes now and then. They do. They're only human. But I never heard of a case where you could say that a judge had positively twisted the law around to—"

That turned the trick. He cursed and snorted and glared at me, and I grinned my insincere doubts, and the story finally came out.

"Me and 'Flogger' Rork was on the road together some years ago, with a gun apiece and a couple big handkerchiefs to hide our mugs behind when we needed to. All-night grease-joints was our meat, and we done ourselves pretty well. We'd knock over a couple a night some nights. We'd drift into them separate at three or four in the morning, not letting on we knew each other, and stall over coffee and sinkers until we was alone with the guy behind the counter. Then we'd flash the rods on him, take what was in the damper, and slide on. No big hauls, you understand, but a steady, reliable income.

"We work that way for a few months, and then I get an idea for a new racket—and it's a darb! Flogger—he's an unimaginative sort of jobbie—can't see it at first. But I keep jawing at him until he gives in and agrees to take a whirl at it.

"You never seen Flogger Rork, did you? I thought not. Well, he's a good guy—what 'Limey' Pine used to call a 'bene cove'—but he ain't no flower to look at. I seen a cartoon of a burglar once in a newspaper during one of these crime waves, and that's the only time I ever seen a face like Flogger's. A good guy—but we had to be careful how we moved around, because bulls had a habit of picking us up just on account of his face. Me—nobody hadn't ever took me for a lamb, myself; though alongside of Flogger I look pretty sweet.

"These mugs of ours had been handicaps to us so far, but now under my new scheme we're going to cash in on them.

"We was in the Middle West at the time. We blow into the next burg on our list, look the main drag over, and go to work. Our guns are ditched down under a pile of rocks near the jungle.

"We make a drug-store. There's two nice little boys in it. I plant myself in front of one of them, with one hand in my coat pocket, and Flogger does the same with the other.

"'Come through,' we tells 'em.

"Without a squawk, one of 'em pushes down the 'No Sale' key of the damper, scoops out every nickel that's in it, and passes it over to Flogger.

"'Lay down behind the counter and don't be too much in a hurry about getting up,' we tell them next.

"They do as they're told, and me and Flogger go on out and about our business.

"The next day we push over two more stores and move on to the next town. Every town we hit we give our new racket a couple of whirls, and it goes nice. Having an ace up our sleeves, we can take chances that otherwise would have been foolish—we can pull a couple or even three jobs a day without waiting for the rumpus from the first one to die down.

"Pickings were pretty them days!

"Then, one afternoon in a fresh burg, we push over a garage, a pawnshop and a shoe store, and we get picked up.

"The bulls that nabbed us was loaded for bear, but—outside of running until we saw it was no use—we went along with them as nice as you please. When they frisked us they found the money from that day's jobs, but that was all. The rest was cached where we knew it would be when we wanted it. And our guns was still under that pile of stones three States away. We didn't have no use for them any more.

"The guys we had stuck up that afternoon came in to look us over, and they all identified us right away. As one of 'em said there was no forgettin' our faces. But we sat tight and said nothing. We knew where we stood and we were satisfied.

"After a couple days they let us have a mouthpiece. We picked out a kid whose diploma hadn't been with him long enough to collect any dust yet, but he looked like he wouldn't throw us down; and he didn't have to know much law for us. Then we laid around and took jail life easy.

"A few days of that, and they yank us into court. We let things run along for a while without fightin' back, until the right time came. Then our kid mouthpiece gets up and springs our little joker on them.

"His clients, he says, meaning me and Flogger, are perfectly willing to plead guilty to begging. But there is nothing to hold them for robbery on. They were in need of funds, and they went into three business establishments and asked for money. They had no weapons. The evidence doesn't show that they made any threats. Whatever motives may have prompted the persons in the stores to hand over the contents of the various cash registers to oblige them—the kid says—has no bearing on the matter. The evidence is plain. His clients asked for money and it was given to them. Begging, certainly—and so his clients are liable to sentences of 30 days or so in the county jail for vagrancy. But robbery—no!

"Well, son, it was a riot! I thought the beak was going to bust something. He's a big bloated hick with a red face and a pair of nose-pinchers. His face turns purple now, and the cheaters slide down his nose three times in five minutes. The district attorney does a proper war dance with the whoops and all. But we had 'em!"

The old man stopped with an air of finality. I waited a while, but he didn't resume the story, if there were, indeed, any more to it; so I prodded him.

"I don't see where that proves your contention," I said. "There's no using of the law as a weapon there."

"Wait, sonny, wait," he promised. "You'll see before I'm through ... They put their witnesses back on the stand again, then. But there was nothing to it. None of 'em had seen any weapons, and none of 'em couldn't say we had threatened 'em. They said things about our looks, but it ain't a crime to be ugly.

"They shut up shop for the day, then, and chased me and Flogger back to the jail. And we went back as happy a pair as you ever seen. We had the world by the tail with a downhill pull, and we liked it. Thirty days, or even sixty, in the county jail on a vag charge didn't mean nothing to us. We'd had that happen to us before, and got over it.

"We were happy—but that came from the ignorance of our trustin' natures. We thought maybe a court was a place where justice was done after all; where right was right; and where things went accordin' to the law. We'd been in trouble with the law before, plenty, but this was different—we had the law on our side this time; and we counted on it stickin' with us. But—"

"Well, anyway, they take us back over to court after a few more days. And as soon as I get a slant at the beak and the district attorney I get sort of a chill up my back. They got mean lights in their eyes, like a coupla kids that had put tacks on a chair and was a-waiting for somebody to sit on them. Maybe, I think, they've rigged things up so's they can slip us two or three, or even six, months on vag charges. But I didn't suspect half of it!

"Say, you've heard this chatter about how slow the courts are, haven't you? Well, let me tell you, nothing in the world ever moved any faster than that court that morning. Before we had got fixed in our chairs, almost, things was humming.

"Our kid mouthpiece is bouncing up and down continuous, trying to get a word in. But not a chance! Every time he opens his mouth the beak cracks down on him and shuts him up; even threatening to throw him out and fine him in the bargain if he don't keep quiet.

"The man we'd gone up against in the garage was the proprietor, but the ones in the hock shop and the shoe store were just hirelings. So they leave the garage man out of the game. But they put the other two in the dock, charged with grand larceny, have 'em plead guilty, sentence 'em to five years apiece, and suspend the sentences before you could shift a chew from one cheek to the other.

"'If,' the beak says in answer to our mouthpiece's squawk, 'your clients simply asked for the money and these men gave it to them, then these two men are guilty of theft, since the money belonged to their employers. There is nothing for the court to do, therefore but to find them guilty of grand larceny and sentence them to five years each in the state prison. But the evidence tends to show that these men were actuated simply by an overwhelming desire to help two of their fellow men; that they were induced to steal the money simply by an ungovernable impulse to charity. And the court, therefore, feels that it is justified in exercising its legal privilege of leniency, and suspending their sentences.'

"Me and Flogger don't understand what's being done to us right away, but our mouthpiece does, and as soon as I get a look at him I know it's pretty bad. He's sort of gasping.

"The rest of the dirty work takes longer, but there's no stopping it. This old buzzard of a judge has our charges changed to 'receiving stolen property'—a felony in that state; we are convicted on two counts, and he slips us ten years in the big house on each, the hitches to run end to end.

"And does that old buzzard feel that the court should exercise its legal privilege of leniency and suspend our sentences? Fat chance! Me and Flogger goes over!"

HIS BROTHER'S KEEPER

I knew what a lot of people said about Loney but he was always swell to me. Ever since I remember he was swell to me and I guess I would have liked him just as much even if he had been just somebody else instead of my brother; but I was glad he was not just somebody else.

He was not like me. He was slim and would have looked swell in any kind of clothes you put on him, only he always dressed classy and looked like he had stepped right out of the bandbox even when he was just loafing around the house, and he had slick hair and the whitest teeth you ever saw and long, thin, clean-looking fingers. He looked like the way I remembered my father, only better-looking. I took more after Ma's folks, the Malones, which was funny because Loney was the one that was named after them. Malone Bolan. He was smart as they make them, too. It was no use trying to put anything over on him and maybe that was what some people had against him, only that was kind of hard to fit in with Pete Gonzalez.

Pete Gonzalez not liking Loney used to bother me sometimes because he was a swell guy, too, and he was never trying to put anything over on anybody. He had two fighters and a wrestler named Kilchak and he always sent them in to do the best they could, just like Loney sent me in. He was the topnotch manager in our part of the country and a lot of people said there was no better anywhere, so I felt pretty good about him wanting to handle me, even if I did say no.

It was in the hall leaving Tubby White's gym that I ran into him that afternoon and he said, "Hello, Kid, how's it?" moving his cigar further over in a corner of his mouth so he could talk.

"Hello. All right."

94

He looked me up and down, squinting on account of the smoke from his cigar. "Going to take this guy Saturday?"

"I guess so."

He looked me up and down again like he was weighing me in. His eyes were little enough anyhow and when he squinted like that you could hardly see them at all. "How old are you, Kid?"

"Going on nineteen."

"And you'll weigh about a hundred and sixty," he said.

"Sixty-seven and a half. I'm growing pretty fast."

"Ever see this guy you're fighting Saturday?"

"No."

"He's plenty tough."

I grinned and said, "I guess he is."

"And plenty smart."

I said, "I guess he is," again.

He took his cigar out of his mouth and scowled at me and said like he was sore at me, "You know you got no business in the ring with him, don't you?" Before I could think up anything to say he stuck the cigar back in his mouth and his face and his voice changed. "Why don't you let me handle you, Kid? You got the stuff. I'll handle you right, build you up, not use you up, and you'll be good for a long trip."

"I couldn't do that," I said. "Loney taught me all I know and—"

"Taught you what?" Pete snarled. He looked mad again. "If you think you been taught anything at all you just take a look at your mug in the next looking-glass you come across." He took the cigar out of his mouth and spit out a piece of tobacco that had come loose. "Only eighteen years old and ain't been fighting a year and look at the mug on him!"

I felt myself blushing. I guess I was never any beauty but, like Pete said, I had been hit in the face a lot and I guess my face showed it. I said, "Well, of course, I'm not a boxer."

"And that's the God's truth," Pete said. "And why ain't you?"

"I don't know. I guess it's just not my way of fighting."

"You could learn. You're fast and you ain't dumb. What's this stuff getting you? Every week Loney sends you in against some guy you're not ready for yet and you soak up a lot of fists and—"

"I win, don't I?" I said.

"Sure you win—so far—because you're young and tough and got the moxie and can hit, but I wouldn't want to pay for winning what you're paying, and I wouldn't want any of my boys to. I seen kids—maybe some of them as promising as you—go along the way you're going, and I seen what was left of them a couple years later. Take my word for it, Kid, you'll do better than that with me."

"Maybe you're right," I said, "and I'm grateful to you and all that, but I couldn't leave Loney. He—"

"I'll give Loney a piece of change for your contract, even if you ain't got one with him."

"No, I'm sorry, I—I couldn't."

Pete started to say something and stopped and his face began to get red. The door of Tubby's office had opened and Loney was coming out. Loney's face was white and you could hardly see his lips because they were so tight together, so I knew he had heard us talking.

He walked up close to Pete, not even looking at me once, and said, "You chiseling dago rat."

Pete said, "I only told him what I told you when I made you the offer last week."

Loney said, "Swell. So now you've told everybody. So now you can tell 'em about this." He smacked Pete across the mouth with the back of his hand.

I moved over a little because Pete was a lot bigger than Loney, but Pete just said, "O. K., pal, maybe you won't live forever. Maybe you won't live forever even if Big Jake don't never get hep to the missus."

Loney swung at him with a fist this time but Pete was backing away down the hall and Loney missed him by about a foot and a half, and when Loney started after him Pete turned and ran toward the gym.

Loney came back to me grinning and not looking mad any more. He could change that way quicker than anybody you ever saw. He put an arm around my shoulders and said, "The chiseling dago rat. Let's blow." Outside he turned me around to look at the sign advertising the fights. "There you are, Kid. I don't blame him for wanting you. There'll be a lot of 'em wanting you before you're through."

It did look swell,   *Kid Bolan vs. Sailor Perelman*, in red letters that were bigger than any of the other names and up at the top of the card. That was the first time I ever had had my name at the top. I thought, I'm going to have it there like that all the time now and maybe in New York sometime, but I just grinned at Loney without saying anything and we went on home.

Ma was away visiting my married sister in Pittsburgh and we had a nigger woman named Susan taking care of the house for us and after she washed up the supper dishes and went home Loney went to the telephone and I could hear him talking low.

I wanted to say something to him when he came back but I was afraid I would say the wrong thing because Loney might think I was trying to butt into his business, and before I could find a safe way to start the doorbell rang.

Loney went to the door. It was Mrs. Schiff, like I had a hunch it would be, because she had come over the first night Ma was away.

She came in laughing, with Loney's arm around her waist, and said, "Hello, Champ," to me.

I said, "Hello," and shook hands with her.

I liked her, I guess, but I guess I was kind of afraid of her. I mean not only afraid of her on Loney's account but in a different way. You know, like sometimes when you were a kid and you found yourself all alone in a strange neighborhood on the other side of town. There was nothing you could see to be downright afraid of but you kept halfway expecting something. It was something like that. She was awful pretty but there was something kind of wild-looking about her. I don't mean wild-looking like some floozies you see; I mean almost like an animal, like she was always on the watch for something. It was like she was hungry. I mean just her eyes and maybe her mouth because you could not call her skinny or anything or fat either.

Loney got out a bottle of whisky and glasses and they had a drink. I stalled around for a few minutes just being polite and then said I guessed I was tired and I said good night to them and took my magazine upstairs to my room. Loney was beginning to tell her about his run-in with Pete Gonzalez when I went upstairs.

After I got undressed I tried to read but I kept worrying about Loney. It was this Mrs. Schiff that Pete made the crack about in the afternoon. She was the wife of Big Jake Schiff, the boss of our ward, and a lot of people must have known about her running around with Loney on the side. Anyhow Pete knew about it and he and Big Jake were pretty good friends besides him now having something to pay Loney back for. I wished Loney would cut it out. He could have had a lot of other girls and Big Jake was nobody to have trouble with, even leaving aside the pull he had down at the City Hall. Every time I tried to read I would get to thinking things like that so finally I gave it up and went to sleep pretty early, even for me.

That was a Monday. Tuesday night when I got home from the movies she was waiting in the vestibule. She had on a long coat but no hat, and she looked pretty excited.

"Where's Loney?" she asked, not saying hello or anything.

"I don't know. He didn't say where he was going."

"I've got to see him," she said. "Haven't you any idea where he'd be?"

"No, I don't know where he is."

"Do you think he'll be late?"

I said, "I guess he usually is."

She frowned at me and then she said, "I've got to see him. I'll wait a little while anyhow." So we went back to the dining-room.

She kept her coat on and began to walk around the room looking at things but without paying much attention to them. I asked her if she wanted a drink and she said, "Yes," sort of absent-minded, but when I started to get it for her she took hold of the lapel of my coat and said, "Listen, Eddie, will you tell me something? Honest to God?"

I said, "Sure," feeling kind of embarrassed looking in her face like that, "if I can."

"Is Loney really in love with me?"

That was a tough one. I could feel my face getting redder and redder. I wished the door would open and Loney would come in. I wished a fire would break out or something.

She jerked my lapel. "Is he?"

I said, "I guess so. I guess he is, all right."

"Don't you know?"

I said, "Sure, I know, but Loney don't ever talk to me about things like that. Honest, he don't."

She bit her lip and turned her back on me. I was sweating. I spent as long a time as I could in the kitchen getting the whisky and things. When I went back in the dining-room she had sat down and was putting lip-stick on her mouth. I set the whisky down on the table beside her.

She smiled at me and said, "You're a nice boy, Eddie. I hope you win a million fights. When do you fight again?"

I had to laugh at that. I guess I had been going around thinking that everybody in the world knew I was going to fight Sailor Perelman that Saturday just because it was my first main event. I guess that is the way you get a swelled head. I said, "This Saturday."

"That's fine," she said, and looked at her wrist-watch. "Oh, why doesn't he come? I've got to be home before Jake gets there." She jumped up. "Well, I can't wait any longer. I shouldn't have stayed this long. Will you tell Loney something for me?"

"Sure."

"And not another soul?"

"Sure."

She came around the table and took hold of my lapel again. "Well, listen. You tell him that somebody's been talking to Jake about—about us. You tell him we've got to

98

be careful, Jake'd kill both of us. You tell him I don't think Jake knows for sure yet, but we've got to be careful. Tell Loney not to phone me and to wait here till I phone him tomorrow afternoon. Will you tell him that?"

"Sure."

"And don't let him do anything crazy."

I said, "I won't." I would have said anything to get it over with.

She said, "You're a nice boy, Eddie," and kissed me on the mouth and went out of the house.

I did not go to the door with her. I looked at the whisky on the table and thought maybe I ought to take the first drink of my life, but instead I sat down and thought about Loney. Maybe I dozed off a little but I was awake when he came home and that was nearly two o'clock.

He was pretty tight. "What the hell are you doing up?" he said.

I told him about Mrs. Schiff and what she told me to tell him.

He stood there in his hat and overcoat until I had told it all, then he said, "That chiseling dago rat," kind of half under his breath and his face began to get like it got when he was mad.

"And she said you mustn't do anything crazy."

"Crazy?" He looked at me and kind of laughed. "No, I won't do anything crazy. How about you scramming off to bed?"

I said, "All right," and went upstairs.

The next morning he was still in bed when I left for the gym and he had gone out before I got home. I waited supper for him until nearly seven o'clock and then ate it by myself. Susan was getting sore because it was going to be late before she got through. Maybe he stayed out all night but he looked all right when he came in Tubby's the next afternoon to watch me work out, and he was making jokes and kidding along with the fellows hanging around there just like he had nothing at all on his mind.

He waited for me to dress and we walked over home together. The only thing that was kind of funny, he asked me, "How do you feel, Kid?" That was kind of funny because he knew I always felt all right. I guess I never even had a cold all my life.

I said, "All right."

"You're working good," he said. "Take it easy tomorrow. You want to be rested up for this baby from Providence. Like that chiseling dago rat said, he's plenty tough and plenty smart."

I said, "I guess he is. Loney, do you think Pete really tipped Big Jake off about—"

"Forget it," he said. "Hell with 'em." He poked my arm. "You got nothing to worry about but how you're going to be in there Saturday night."

"I'll be all right."

"Don't be too sure," he said. "Maybe you'll be lucky to get a draw."

I stopped still in the street, I was so surprised. Loney never talked like that about any of my fights before. He was always saying, "Don't worry about how tough this mug looks, just go in and knock him apart," or something like that.

I said, "You mean—?"

He took hold of my arm to start me walking again. "Maybe I overmatched you this time, Kid. This sailor's pretty good. He can box and he hits a lot harder than anybody you been up against so far."

"Oh, I'll be all right," I said.

"Maybe," he said, scowling straight ahead. "Listen, what do you think about what Pete said about you needing more boxing?"

"I don't know. I don't ever pay any attention much to what anybody says but you."

"Well, what do you think about it now?" he asked.

"Sure, I'd like to learn to box better, I guess."

He grinned at me without moving his lips much. "You're liable to get some fine lessons from this Sailor whether you want 'em or not. But no kidding, suppose I told you to box him instead of tearing in, would you do it? I mean for the experience, even if you didn't make much of a showing that way."

I said, "Don't I always fight the way you tell me?"

"Sure you do. But suppose it meant maybe losing this once but learning something?"

"I want to win, of course," I said, "but I'll do anything you tell me. Do you want me to fight him that way?"

"I don't know," he said. "We'll see."

Friday and Saturday I just loafed around. Friday I tried to find somebody to go out and shoot pheasants with but all I could find was Bob Kirby and I was tired of listening to him make the same jokes over and over, so I changed my mind and stayed home.

Loney came home for supper and I asked him what the odds were on our fight.

He said, "Even money. You got a lot of friends."

"Are we betting?" I asked.

"Not yet. Maybe if the price gets better. I don't know."

I wished he had not been so afraid I was going to lose but I thought it might sound kind of conceited if I said anything about it, so I just went on eating.

We had a swell house that Saturday night. The armory was packed and we got a pretty good hand when we went in the ring. I felt fine and I guess Dick Cohen, who was going to be in my corner with Loney, felt fine too, because he looked like he was trying to keep from grinning. Only Loney looked kind of worried, not enough that you would notice it unless you knew him as well as I did, but I could notice it.

"I'm all right," I told him. A lot of fighters say they feel uncomfortable waiting for their fight to start but I always feel fine.

Loney said, "Sure you are," and slapped me on my back. "Listen, Kid," he said, and cleared his throat. He put his mouth over close to my ear so nobody else would hear him. "Listen, Kid, maybe—maybe you better box him like we said. O. K.?"

I said, "O. K."

"And don't let those mugs out front yell you into anything. You're doing the fighting up there."

I said, "O. K."

The first couple of rounds were kind of fun in a way because this was new stuff to me, this moving around him on my toes and going in and out with my hands high. Of course I had done some of that with fellows in the gym but not in the ring before and not with anybody that was as good at it as he was. He was pretty good and had it all over me both of those rounds but nobody hurt anybody else.

But in the first minute of the third he got to my jaw with a honey of a right cross and then whammed me in the body twice fast with his left. Pete and Loney had not been kidding when they said he could hit. I forgot about boxing and went in pumping with both hands, driving him all the way across the ring before he tied me up in a clinch. Everybody yelled so I guess it looked pretty good but I only really hit him once; he took the rest of them on his arms. He was the smartest fighter I had ever been up against.

By the time Pop Agnew broke us I remembered I was supposed to be boxing so I went back to that, but Perelman was going faster and I spent most of the rest of the round trying to keep his left out of my face.

"Hurt you?" Loney asked when I was back in my corner.

"Not yet," I said, "but he can hit."

In the fourth I stopped another right cross with my eye and a lot of lefts with other parts of my face and the fifth round was still tougher. For one thing, the eye he had hit me in was almost shut by that time and for another thing I guess he had me pretty well figured out. He went around and around me, not letting me get set.

"How do you feel?" Loney asked when he and Dick were working on me after that round. His voice was funny, like he had a cold.

I said, "All right." It was hard to talk much because my lips were puffed out.

"Cover up more," Loney said.

I shook my head up and down to say I would.

"And don't pay any attention to those mugs out front."

I had been too busy with Sailor Perelman to pay much attention to anybody else but when we came out for the sixth round I could hear people hollering things like, "Go in and fight him, Kid," and, "Come on, Kid, go to work on this guy," and, "What are you waiting for, Kid?" so I guessed they had been hollering like that all along. Maybe that had something to do with it or maybe I just wanted to show Loney that I was still all right so he would not worry about me. Anyway, along toward the last part of the round, when Perelman jarred me with another one of those right crosses that I was having so much trouble with, I got down low and went in after him. He hit me some but not enough to keep me away and, even if he did take care of most of my punches, I got in a couple of good ones and I could tell that he felt them. And when he tied me up in a clinch I knew he could do it because he was smarter than me and not because he was stronger.

"What's the matter with you?" he growled in my ear. "Are you gone nuts?" I never liked to talk in the ring so I just grinned to myself without saying anything and kept trying to get a hand loose.

Loney scowled at me when I sat down after that round. "What's the matter with you?" he said. "Didn't I tell you to box him?" He was awful pale and his voice was hoarse.

I said, "All right, I will."

Dick Cohen began to curse over on the side I could not see out of. He did not seem to be cursing anybody or anything, just cursing in a low voice until Loney told him to shut up.

I wanted to ask Loney what I ought to do about that right cross but, with my mouth the way it was, talking was a lot of work and, besides, my nose was stopped up and I had to use my mouth for breathing, so I kept quiet. Loney and Dick worked harder on me than they had between any of the other rounds. When Loney crawled out of the ring just before the gong he slapped me on the shoulder and said in a sharp voice, "Now box."

I went out and boxed. Perelman must have got to my face thirty times that round; anyway it felt like he did, but I kept on trying to box him. It seemed like a long round.

I went back to my corner not feeling exactly sick but like I might be going to get sick, and that was funny because I could not remember being hit in the stomach to amount to anything. Mostly Perelman had been working on my head. Loney looked a lot sicker than I felt. He looked so sick I tried not to look at him and I felt kind of ashamed of making a bum out of him by letting this Perelman make a monkey out of me like he was doing.

"Can you last it out?" Loney asked.

When I tried to answer him I found that I could not move my lower lip because the inside of it was stuck on a broken tooth. I put a thumb up to it and Loney pushed my glove away and pulled the lip loose from the tooth.

Then I said, "Sure. I'll get the hang of it pretty soon."

Loney made a queer gurgling kind of noise down in his throat and all of a sudden put his face up close in front of mine so that I had to stop looking at the floor and look at him. His eyes were like you think a hophead's are. "Listen, Kid," he says, his voice sounding cruel and hard, almost like he hated me. "To hell with this stuff. Go in and get that mug. What the hell are you boxing for? You're a fighter. Get in there and fight."

I started to say something and then stopped, and I had a goofy idea that I would like to kiss him or something and then he was climbing through the ropes and the gong rang.

I did like Loney said and I guess I took that round by a pretty good edge. It was swell, fighting my own way again, going in banging away with both hands, not swinging or anything silly like that, just shooting them in short and hard, leaning from side to side to get everything from the ankles up into them. He hit me of course but I figured he was not likely to be able to hit me any harder than he had in the other rounds and I had stood up under that, so I was not worrying about it now. Just before the gong rang I threw him out of a clinch and when it rang I had him covering up in a corner.

It was swell back in my corner. Everybody was yelling all around except Loney and Dick and neither of them said a single word to me. They hardly looked at me, just at the parts they were working on and they were rougher with me than they ever were before. You would have thought I was a machine they were fixing up. Loney was not looking sick any more. I could tell he was excited because his face was set hard and still. I like to remember him that way, he was awful good-looking. Dick was whistling between his teeth very low while he doused my head with a sponge.

I got Perelman sooner than I expected, in the ninth. The first part of the round was his because he came out moving fast and left-handing me and making me look pretty silly, I guess, but he could not keep it up and I got in under one of his lefts and cracked him on the chin with a left hook, the first time I had been able to lay one on his head the way I wanted to. I knew it was a good one even before his head went back and I threw six punches at him as fast as I could get them out—left, right, left, right, left, right. He took care of four of them but I got him on the chin again with a right and just above his trunks with another, and when his knees bent a little and he tried to clinch I pushed him away and smacked him on the cheek bone with everything I had.

Then Dick Cohen was putting my bathrobe over my shoulders and hugging me and sniffling and cursing and laughing all at the same time, and across the ring they were propping Perelman up on his stool.

"Where's Loney?" I asked.

Dick looked around. "I don't know. He was here. Boy, was that a mill!"

Loney caught up to us just as we were going in the dressing-room. "I had to see a fellow," he said. His eyes were bright like he was laughing at something, but he was white as a ghost and he held his lips tight against his teeth even when he grinned kind of lopsided at me and said, "It's going to be a long time before anybody beats you, Kid."

I said I hoped it was. I was awful tired now that it was all over. Usually I get awful hungry after a fight but this time I was just awful tired.

Loney went across to where he had hung his coat and put it on over his sweater, and when he put it on the tail of it caught and I saw he had a gun in his hip pocket. That was funny because I never knew him to carry a gun before and if he had had it in the ring everybody would have been sure to see it when he bent over working on me. I could not ask him about it because there were a lot of people in there talking and arguing.

Pretty soon Perelman came in with his manager and two other men who were strangers to me, so I guessed they had come down from Providence with him too. He was looking straight ahead but the others looked kind of hard at Loney and me and went up to the other end of the room without saying anything. We all dressed in one long room there.

Loney said to Dick, who was helping me, "Take your time. I don't want the Kid to go out till he's cooled off."

Perelman got dressed pretty quick and went out still looking straight ahead. His manager and the two men with him stopped in front of us. The manager was a big man with green eyes like a fish and a dark kind of flat face. He had an accent too, maybe he was a Polack. He said, "Smart boys, huh?"

Loney was standing up with one hand behind him. Dick Cohen put his hands on the back of a chair and kind of leaned over it. Loney said, "I'm smart. The Kid fights the way I tell him to fight."

The manager looked at me and looked at Dick and looked at Loney again and said "M-m-m, so that's the way it is." He thought a minute and said, "That's something to know." Then he pulled his hat down tighter on his head and turned around and went out with the other two men following.

I asked Loney, "What's the matter?"

He laughed but not like it was anything funny. "Bad losers."

"But you've got a gun in—"

He cut me off. "Uh-huh, a fellow asked me to hold it for him. I got to go give it back to him now. You and Dick go on home and I'll see you there in a little while. But don't hurry, because I want you to cool off before you go out. You two take the car, you know where we parked it. Come here, Dick."

He took Dick over in a corner and whispered to him. Dick kept nodding his head up and down and looking more and more scared, even if he did try to hide it when he turned around to me. Loney said, "Be seeing you," and went out.

"What's the matter?" I asked Dick.

He shook his head and said, "It's nothing to worry about," and that was every word I could get out of him.

Five minutes later Bob Kirby's brother Pudge ran in and yelled, "Jees, they shot Loney!"

I shot Loney. If I was not so dumb he would still be alive anyway you figure it. For a long time I blamed it on Mrs. Schiff, but I guess that was just to keep from admitting that it was my own fault. I mean I never thought she actually did the shooting, like the people who said that when he missed the train that they were supposed to go away on together she came back and waited outside the armory and when he came out he told her he had changed his mind and she shot him. I mean I blamed her for lying to him, because it came out that nobody had tipped Big Jake off about her and Loney. Loney had put the idea in her head, telling her about what Pete had said, and she had made up the lie so Loney would go away with her. But if I was not so dumb Loney would have caught that train.

Then a lot of people said Big Jake killed Loney. They said that was why the police never got very far, on account of Big Jake's pull down at the City Hall. It was a fact that he had come home earlier than Mrs. Schiff had expected and she had left a note for him saying that she was running away with Loney, and he could have made it down to the street near the armory where Loney was shot in time to do it, but he could not have got to the railroad station in time to catch their train, and if I was not so dumb Loney would have caught that train.

And the same way if that Sailor Perelman crowd did it, which is what most people including the police thought even if they did have to let them go because they could not find enough evidence against them. If I was not so dumb Loney could have said to me right out, "Listen, Kid, I've got to go away and I've got to have all the money I can scrape up and the best way to do it is to make a deal with Perelman for you to go in the tank and then bet all we got against you." Why, I would have thrown a million fights for Loney, but how could he know he could trust me, with me this dumb?

105

Or I could have guessed what he wanted and I could have gone down when Perelman copped me with that uppercut in the fifth. That would have been easy. Or if I was not so dumb I would have learned to box better and, even losing to Perelman like I would have anyway, I could have kept him from chopping me to pieces so bad that Loney could not stand it any more and had to throw away everything by telling me to stop boxing and go in and fight.

Or even if everything had happened like it did up to then he could still have ducked out at the last minute if I was not so dumb that he had to stick around to look out for me by telling those Providence guys that I had nothing to do with double-crossing them.

I wish I was dead instead of Loney.

Printed in the USA
CPSIA information can be obtained
at www.ICGtesting.com
LVHW091039160824
788360LV00004B/727

9 781773 237770